KILLER SMILE

Jack Monroe's dream was to start a foundation that would encourage architects from poorer families. But to achieve this dream he would need fifty million dollars. So he hooked up with the wealthy Thornhill family. But the Thornhills had more than their share of dirty secrets, and Jack found himself a pawn in a deadly game of murder and deceit. Now, he would need to take the utmost care not to become the architect of his own downfall.

STEVE HAYES
&
DAVID WHITEHEAD

◆

KILLER SMILE

Complete and Unabridged

LINFORD
Leicester

First published in Great Britain

First Linford Edition
published 2011

British Library CIP Data

Hayes, Steve.
  Killer smile. - -
  (Linford mystery library)
  1. Rich people- -Fiction. 2. Family secrets- -
  Fiction. 3. Suspense fiction.
  4. Large type books.
  I. Title II. Series III. Whitehead, David, *1958* –
  823.9'2–dc22

  ISBN 978–1–4448–0926–8

Published by
F. A. Thorpe (Publishing)
Anstey, Leicestershire

Set by Words & Graphics Ltd.
Anstey, Leicestershire
Printed and bound in Great Britain by
T. J. International Ltd., Padstow, Cornwall

This book is printed on acid-free paper

1

It was a fabulous day to die.

Three thousand blossoming pink- and white-flowered cherry trees, a gift from Japan one hundred years earlier to symbolize the arrival of spring and brighten the open area surrounding the Jefferson Memorial, trembled in the gentle breeze blowing off the Tidal Basin. The sky above Potomac Park was a cloudless cornflower blue, the clean dawn air pleasantly mild for late March.

Roy McGowan knew from experience that as the day wore on the park's two halves, west and east, would fill with visitors. They'd come to play tennis or golf, to picnic, bike, swim or hike. They'd visit the memorials or throw bread to the ducks and have their pictures taken beside the reflecting pool.

But for now, at least, the park belonged to him.

Tall and bulky in his NATO-green

Buffalo windbreaker, with a shock of silver hair above a ruddy, good-natured face, McGowan stood with legs spread on the grass about fifty yards behind the famous memorial and drew a satisfied breath. He was a highly successful lobbyist in his late fifties, with the kind of client list his competitors could only dream about. He represented captains of industry and pharmaceutical giants, electric utilities, oil and gas interests and even a couple of Hollywood studio heads. And after spending almost four decades in the business of politics he knew better than most the way things worked in Washington, and that's why he always got results.

Away from The Hill, he was a man of affable temperament and simple pleasures who liked to build and fly model airplanes. He was flying one now.

It was a Eurofighter *Typhoon* with a wingspan of more than three feet, and though this was its maiden flight, he controlled it deftly by means of two tiny joysticks on the Spektrum DX-7 radio system hanging from shoulder straps at his waist.

Under his guidance the airplane thrust skyward, leveled out and then flew in ever-widening circles above the vast, yellow-green grass. From tip to tail the sleek, foam-filled fuselage measured a little less than five feet. With pre-installed navigation lights twinkling from its cropped delta wings, and canards alternately dipping and rising on either side of the cockpit, it looked almost indistinguishable from the real thing, especially from a distance. Only the high, angry whine of its 1750Kv Outrunner brushless motor betrayed the illusion.

McGowan, an expert pilot himself, worked the joysticks mostly by feel. This morning's exercise was merely a test flight, a chance for McGowan to evaluate the fighter's performance and correct any problems. He'd already noticed a minor glitch with the retractable landing gear, but that would be an easy fix. He had a more reliable 9-gram Servo in his cluttered workshop. It would only take a couple of minutes to replace the original.

Determined to put the Eurofighter through its paces, he made a few quick movements with his fingers: full left rudder, full up elevator, just a touch of the right aileron; and the Eurofighter performed a beautiful left flat spin.

He grinned, then neutralized the elevator, did likewise with the aileron and gave the craft just a touch of right rudder. It immediately came out of the maneuver.

Another twitch at the controls and the needle-nosed fighter went rocketing heavenward. It streaked higher and higher until it was just a gray dot in the blue sky; then it performed a lazy loop-the-loop, a victory roll, and finally started another descent.

Deciding to have a little fun, McGowan sent the plane swooping toward the dome of the Jefferson Memorial. Moving at almost one hundred miles an hour, the fighter closed the distance in mere seconds.

Then —

Timing the move to perfection, McGowan pulled the fighter out of its dive just when a collision seemed inevitable. The airplane swept wing-over away from the monument and then came around in another wide circle.

He grinned again, pleased as much with himself as with his latest toy. And so far he'd only been operating on low rates. Once he really got the feel of the craft and switched to high, its performance would be even more impressive. But that was for the future. For now he had one final maneuver to perform — the landing.

He kept the fighter circling overhead for a while, then set up his final approach, making sure to give the nosecone a slight upward angle and the craft itself a little more throttle to help arrest its descent.

At first the fighter responded perfectly. It dropped smoothly toward the short-cropped grass, its shadow darting along beneath it as if tied there by invisible string. But when McGowan tried to lower the landing gear, the plane ignored his command and started to angle skyward instead.

Puzzled, he quickly checked the transmitter's digital screen. The Spektrum DX-7 was a seven-channel computer radio, and he'd taken special care to get the mix between wing type, control surfaces, rudder and everything else just right. Confirming that he'd programmed all the rates correctly, he toggled the joysticks again. But no matter what he did, the aircraft stubbornly ignored his every command.

He examined the transmitter for any signs of malfunction. Nothing. He made sure the transmitter was in the correct PPM modulation mode. It was.

And yet the fighter was apparently flying under its own volition — which was impossible.

Briefly he considered the likelihood of radio or cell phone interference, but that seemed as unlikely as the only other possibility — that two transmitters had somehow locked onto the same frequency at the same time. Even so, he hurriedly scanned his surroundings, confirming that he was alone.

Then a change in the pitch of the motor made him look up again. The Eurofighter was coming out of a wide turn and beginning what looked suspiciously like a bombing run . . . with him as the target.

With growing alarm McGowan watched

as the aircraft halved the distance between them. He still couldn't understand what had caused the malfunction. Model airplanes didn't turn rogue, and yet —

The Eurofighter swept lower, the whine of its motor rising to a scream, warning McGowan that he'd better head for cover. Turning, he started running for the Jefferson Memorial, realizing too late how far away it was.

The Eurofighter streaked after him, its wings, canards, elevons and thrust vector nozzles tipping and tilting frantically as if in anticipation of what was to come. Above the sound of his panting McGowan heard the buzz of the motor coming closer and knew he was never going to outrun the plane.

At the last second he threw himself to the ground.

The airplane roared overhead, missing him by inches, and flew on.

McGowan rolled over and jumped to his feet. Looking up, he saw the Eurofighter making a high, fast circle, sunlight flaring off its gray, back-swept wings.

It was coming for him again.

Panicked, he again started running for the protection of the Jefferson Memorial.

Behind him he heard the spiteful drone of the aircraft's motor, now flat out, rise in pitch, pushing the fighter to top speed —

McGowan glanced back to get a fix on his pursuer — and froze.

The fighter plunged at him like a great gray bird of prey, its wings suddenly rock-steady, its sleek silhouette growing larger, larger —

Seconds later it slammed into his face, smashing through flesh, bone and brain, virtually decapitating him.

Man and machine went down in a bloody sprawl.

Both died at the same time.

★   ★   ★

A few seconds passed and then a figure stepped from behind one of the white Vermont marble columns supporting the dome-roof of the Jefferson Memorial. The shadows of the other columns hid the

8

newcomer's face, but they didn't hide the radio control system the figure had used to override McGowan's transmitter.

Neither did they quite disguise the cool killer smile the figure allowed itself at a job well done.

Satisfied that Roy McGowan was dead, the figure turned and walked unhurriedly away.

2

The small one-story chapel in Oak Hill Cemetery sat among trees and well-groomed hedgerows on a high ridge overlooking the graveyard, which resembled a terraced botanical garden. Built in 1850, it was the only known example of James Renwick's Gothic Revival ecclesiastical design in Washington, D.C.

Today, as rain pelted down on the steeply pitched roof, buttresses and white, cathedral-shaped windows, a funeral had just ended at a nearby grave site. Mourners, umbrellas shielding them from the worst of the downpour, quietly offered their condolences to the grieving young widow and then walked off through the dripping trees and flowing shrubs to their waiting cars.

The widow, Mallory McGowan, accepted them graciously from behind her black veil. A tall, tanned, robust man in his mid-forties approached. Immaculately dressed, he lifted his umbrella enough so she could see his strong handsome face. Mallory recognized him immediately from interviews on television and photographs in the *New York Times* and *Washington Post*. He was Brady Thornhill, a high-profile, charismatic billionaire who had a reputation for always getting what he wanted.

'You don't know me, Mrs. McGowan,' he began. 'But I met your husband several times — '

'I know,' she lied. 'He spoke of you often.'

'I hope it wasn't all negative.'

'On the contrary, Mr. Thornhill, Roy admired you.'

'Then he's on a very short list,' Thornhill said wryly. 'May I escort you to your car?'

She let him dangle for a moment before saying: 'If you don't mind sullying your reputation.'

Brady Thornhill gave her a wolfish smile, his teeth very white against his California tan. 'Mrs Thornhill,' he said, taking her arm, 'I stopped worrying about my reputation when I got kicked out of kindergarten for selling lemonade spiked with gin.'

11

3

If it's true that stand-up comedy is the loneliest job in the world, then Jack Monroe felt like the last man on earth.

He hadn't performed stand-up since college. He hadn't even *thought* about it for years. And yet here he was, standing in the middle of a stage with his hand clutching the microphone and thinking: *What the hell do I say now?*

The spotlights were so harsh that he couldn't see beyond them, and it was all he could do not to screw his eyes shut against their dusty glare. Worse, it was so quiet that he couldn't even be sure if there *was* an audience out there.

Then someone cleared his throat expectantly. Okay, so there *was* an audience. But what was he supposed to say to them? He hadn't come prepared. He'd just been shoved onto the stage and told to get on with it.

The same person coughed again, and

he drew a breath and thought: *I've got to say something.*

'You know,' he began hesitantly, 'I'm not saying I come from a poor family, but when I was a kid we couldn't even afford to pay *attention*.'

Silence.

'We were so poor we used to go to KFC and lick other *people's* fingers.'

More silence.

'Money was a big deal in our house,' he went on, fighting the urge to panic, 'mostly because we never had any. I mean, I knew my folks couldn't afford to give me a bike, so I thought I'd ask God to give me one instead. Then I remembered that God doesn't work that way, so I stole one and asked for forgiveness instead.'

Not a sound.

'Seriously, though, folks, I really *do* need money right now, but it's just not happening for me. No matter where I go or who I ask . . . Then again, I guess I've always been unlucky. Just this afternoon I had to tell my neighbor that *my* dog had killed *his* dog. He said, 'That's impossible! My dog's a Rottweiler. He stands thirty inches at the shoulder and weighs a hundred-thirty pounds.' I said, 'Yeah, I know, but he just choked on my Chihuahua.''

The throat-clearer cleared his throat again.

Jack was dying fast. 'Ever wonder why elevators smell different to midgets?' he asked.

Nothing.

'I really *do* need that money, folks.'

Zip.

Nada.

'Ah well,' he said, finally conceding defeat. 'You know what they say. If at first you don't succeed, then skydiving's not for you.'

A vague shuffling of feet.

'You've been great,' he said, and then walked forward until he fell off the edge of the stage.

★ ★ ★

He woke up with his heart trying to thump its way out of his ribcage. He lay there another moment before he realized he was at home, in bed, and that he'd had another anxiety dream.

He gradually forced his muscles to unclench.

Jeez . . .

He kicked the sheets back and got up. He'd been dreaming all night, and now felt even more exhausted than he had before he'd gone to bed. Too bad; today was an important one for him and he would've preferred to be fresh and sharp for it.

Glad to be up, he stretched, yawned, and padded through the messy, book-cluttered apartment until he reached the kitchen. Dropping a couple of frozen waffles in the toaster, he glanced out the window at the misty early-morning San Francisco skyline, then went into the bathroom and showered.

Jack was in his early thirties, a little above average height with an athletic build. As he screwed his distinctive sea-blue eyes shut against the steaming water he thought again about the dreams and told himself that everything was going to be fine, that he shouldn't worry because he really *could* do this. But no matter how much he tried to bolster his confidence, he knew that today was make or break. He'd exhausted just about every other possibility. Max Harriwell was his last chance. And if Harriwell said no, then he was finished.

He turned off the shower, grabbed a towel and quickly scrub-dried his mid-length, dark-brown hair. He finger-combed it back off his face, then wiped steam off the mirror above the sink and looked himself in the eye. He had a vaguely Italianate look and his pushed-in nose made him look more like a movie heavy than an architect. He wondered if the reason he'd so far failed to secure the money he needed was because he had a face that rich men didn't trust.

He took his time shaving, determined to make the best possible job of it, but when he'd finished his square jaw looked as stubble-dark as when he'd started. Sometimes he wondered if he shouldn't just concede defeat and let his beard grow.

Returning to the bedroom, he put on

his least-creased suit, a dark-blue pin-stripe and knotted a tie about his collar. He seemed unaware of how badly the shamrock-green tie clashed with his suit. Satisfied that he looked as good as he could, he went back into the kitchen, saw a cup of coffee on the counter and took a gulp. It went down cold and sour. Grimacing, he remembered that he'd made it the previous evening and then forgotten about it.

Jesus, was that a bad omen?

He was still considering that as he took one of the waffles out of the toaster and bit into it. The waffle was ice cold, too, and he realized he'd forgotten to plug the toaster in.

Ah well, he wasn't hungry anyway. Taking a Pure Protein shortcake bar from the bread-box he headed for the front door. He'd stuck a Post-It note there to remind himself about the meeting today — as if even *he*, the original absent-minded professor could forget it.

MAX HARRIWELL — 10:30 — MAVERICK CLUB

LAST HURRAH
MUST WIN HIM OVER
YOU CAN DO IT!

Jack stared at the sticker for a long moment, repeating those last four words under his breath and trying to ignore the pessimist inside him who kept saying: *Yeah, right!*

He was still repeating the mantra when he left his brownstone apartment on Geary Street, his mind focusing now on the man he was due to meet. Max Harriwell was a tough, hard-nosed businessman who enjoyed crushing and belittling his opposition. He had interests everywhere, many of them in recession-proof areas like aerospace, defense, energy supply, healthcare, entertainment and banking.

Wondering how he could win such an important man over, Jack started across the street. A horn blared angrily to his right and he had to leap out of the path of an oncoming Hyundai Accent. He turned to the driver, held his hands palms-out and mouthed, *Sorry*. The angry woman behind the wheel yelled an obscenity at him and flipped him the bird.

Undaunted, he made it to the corner of O'Farrell and Van Ness in one piece and caught the Muni to Stillman Street. Ten minutes later he reached his destination, a converted red-brick warehouse that now provided office space for a variety of small businesses, including his own modest architectural consultancy.

Like his apartment, the mid-sized office was also a mess, despite the best efforts of Jack's secretary, Jilly Ingram, to keep everything neat. Desks, shelves and just about every other flat surface available were filled to danger level with blueprints and books on architecture.

As he entered the single room Jack saw that Jilly was trying to unjam the Xerox machine and not having much luck. She pulled her toner-smudged hand out of the copier and straightened up as he went to the chessboard on the corner filing cabinet and studied it intently. Chess was as much a passion for him as it was for her and the game between them had been progressing slowly for weeks now, one move and one counter-move each day. Before she'd left the previous evening, Jilly had opted to move her white knight to his king's bishop 3. Sneaky.

'We can design space probes and bombs that fly around corners, but we can't make a copier that doesn't jam,' Jilly said by way of a greeting. She was almost ten years younger than Jack, slim and naturally curvy, with a pretty, oval face framed by long, dark-brown hair. 'Why is that?'

'It's a conspiracy,' he said, continuing to study the board.

'Between . . . ?'

'Companies making copiers and companies selling extended warranties.'

'Does that include copiers bought off the back of a truck?' she asked pointedly.

'Your Honor,' Jack said in his best tough guy voice, 'I swear I dunno nuttin' 'bout no trucks!'

Jilly chuckled and continued trying to free up the copier.

Jack finally made his counter-move, advancing his queen's knight pawn two squares forward to end up at QK4,

20

thinking: *Hah! Bet you never saw that coming.* 'Your move,' he told her smugly.

She joined him. And after a quick glance at his move, immediately advanced her own queen's knight to his queen's bishop 3, threatening his pawn. 'Hah,' she said. 'Bet you thought I didn't see *that* coming.'

Irked, he had no answer.

Jilly, seeing the Protein bar poking out of his breast pocket, pulled it out and wagged it under his nose. 'Forget to plug the toaster in again?'

He grabbed the bar back and sized her up. She was wearing a *Fight Breast Cancer* T-shirt and a pair of old jeans that hugged her hips. 'Why aren't you wearing a dress?' he demanded. 'Today's Tuesday, remember? You have to drive me to my meeting this morning.'

'Silly me. Forgot my chauffeur's uniform.'

'I'm serious, Jilly. Harriwell comes from old money. He owns banks and a baseball team. I have to make a good impression.'

'You will. You've been paroled.' She handed him a letter with a *Superior*

Court of *California, County of San Francisco* heading.

He quickly scanned it and then punched the air. 'Yesss!'

'You got away with it this time, Jack. But they'll still suspend your license for two years if you get another ticket within the next twelve months.'

'Piece of cake,' he replied. Then, seeing her look of catching the skepticism: 'What, you don't think I can do it?'

'When you're mind isn't wandering you can.'

'In case you've forgotten, I'm a professor. Professor's minds are *supposed* to wander.'

'Only in Disney movies. In real life, they're accidents waiting to happen.' She gave him a closer look and the expression in her wide hazel eyes softened noticeably . . . except that Jack, *being* Jack, failed to notice it. 'Seriously, boss, you have to pay more attention to what's going on around you, or one day you'll get killed.'

He frowned, but had no come-back. She was right. Just as she was right about most things. He knew that and he also knew that he wouldn't get too far in life without her. Impulsively he pecked her on the cheek. 'I will. Promise. By the way,' he added, striking a pose, 'how do I look?'

Jilly checked him out. When she came to his tie she made a face. 'Hang on.'

Opening her desk drawer, she spread out the four new ties inside. Marked on each wrapper was the suit they matched. Choosing the one that would go best with his navy pinstripe, she turned back to him.

His eyes widened. 'Where'd you get *that?*'

'I bought it for my boyfriend,' she lied. 'But I'm sure he won't mind, considering Mr. Harriwell's our last hope.' She stood in front of him, removed his green tie, flipped the replacement over his head, under his collar and then started knotting it. As she worked, she couldn't help admiring him. But when he returned her look and gave her a comical flip of his eyebrows, she knew he had absolutely no idea what he meant to her.

'Good luck, boss.'

'You mean lower my principles?' he asked sourly.

'I mean at least hear the old fart *out*.'

He grinned and left the office. She stood there, wondering why she'd had to fall for the one man who thought of her as a kid sister, then turned back to the jammed photocopier.

Unexpectedly, Jack poked his head back around the door. 'I didn't know you had a boyfriend.'

'You would if your head wasn't up your butt,' Jilly said. 'Now get going or you'll be late.'

★   ★   ★

Stillwell Street ran parallel to 1-80, which was elevated along this stretch. The people who lived and worked in the area parked their cars in a fenced lot within its shadow. Jack entered the lot and headed for the tarp-covered car he'd had to forego since his last traffic violation. He pulled the tarp away, revealing a newly-waxed '69 Camaro convertible, and grinned.

'Hiya, baby,' he murmured.

The car was another of his four major passions, ranking well ahead of chess and football but lagging sadly behind his real dream — the Monroe Foundation for Architects.

He looked lovingly at the vintage Camaro's sleek lines. It was a lustrous royal blue, with two wide white stripes running from grille to windshield, either side of the raised cowl-induction hood. Finally he slid behind the wheel and gunned the 302-CID V-8 engine. The sound of the rumbling pipes was heavenly.

Attracted by the noise, a bewhiskered old man in a greasy gray shirt over an equally greasy red t-shirt, shambled up. 'Jack's back!' he yelled above the roar, and then cackled.

Jack grinned and cut the engine. 'How much do I owe you for the wax job?'

The old man pushed the *Giants* baseball cap back off his lined forehead. His name was Garland Hicks, and he watched over the lot twelve hours day from the tiny booth he virtually lived in.

'Not me,' he said. 'Jilly. She was in here bright and early. Hand-rubbed it herself.'

'You're kidding? Man, what a sweetheart.'

'You oughta marry that girl,' Hicks said. 'Chicks who love old muscle cars and football are an endangered species.'

'So are bachelors,' Jack replied. He drove off, his mind already fixated on the meeting that lay ahead of him. Financially, it was a matter of life or death.

4

The Maverick Club, on John Street, began life in 1887 as the San Francisco *pied-à-terre* of the copper magnate Joseph Astor Whitney. One of the earliest and finest brownstones to grace the Bay area skyline, it was also one of the few to survive the earthquake of 1906. Now it was an exclusive gentlemen's club that offered peace, privacy and complete discretion for those who could afford it. No cameras, no phones and certainly no women were allowed.

Due to heavy traffic, Jack arrived only minutes before his appointment. A bellboy led him up a grand, sweeping staircase to a long room with wood-paneled walls and a vaulted ceiling.

Along the way he couldn't help gawking at the opulent surroundings. Everything about the place spoke of money, from the rare first editions that lined the bookcases — titles by the likes of Ptolemy, Dürer, Philip Lutley Sclater and others — to the paintings that overlooked the antique Baktiari carpets and Afshar rugs. The air smelled of fine cigars and lavender polish. Huge button-studded leather sofas and chairs were positioned in corners and around fireplaces and chunky coffee tables, and everywhere he looked he saw overweight men with bald heads or white hair, smoking cigars or sipping fine cognac, reading the *Wall Street Journal* or conversing in undertones.

The man Jack had come to see sat surveying everyone from a corner chair at the rear of the room. Thanks to the light coming through the French windows behind him, he was a silhouette at first. Then, as Jack drew closer, he got his first look at the man who, this day, could make or break him.

Max Harriwell was a poorly-preserved seventy, whose face wore the loose, saggy skin of a once-fat man who'd lost too much weight. His skin was dry and sallow, like parchment, his small mouth pinched in to either side by slack jowls;

but his blue eyes were still hard and sharp, like polished buttons. His hair was thin and combed over, and he had the sour, disappointed look of someone who'd peeled an orange only to find a lemon under the skin.

The bellboy stopped and introduced the two men. 'Mr Harriwell . . . Professor Monroe.'

Jack offered Harriwell his hand. 'Thanks for sparing me a few minutes, sir.'

Harriwell grudgingly shook hands. His grip was soft and clammy; his nails beautifully manicured. 'Just make sure they're productive,' he said.

He gestured at the chair opposite him and Jack sank into the soft, creaking leather. Harriwell opened the lid of the humidor on the low table between them and tilted it for Jack's inspection. 'Cigar?'

'No thank you, sir.'

Harriwell shrugged, selected one for himself, snipped off the end and lit up. 'No vices?' he asked.

'Just vintage muscle cars and chess.'

'Never had any use for either.'

Jack felt his mouth tighten as he

29

studied the man through the curling smoke.

'First rule of business,' said Harriwell. 'Never let your adversary know what you're thinking.'

'I don't really think of you as an adversary, sir,' Jack said diplomatically.

'Rule number two,' said Harriwell. 'Never present a weak front. It leaves only compromise. And from what I've heard, you don't like compromising.'

'I don't know who you've been talking to, sir, but I would say it all depends on the compromise.' He reached for the carafe on the table and poured himself a half-glass of water.

Watching his every movement, Harriwell exhaled a veil of smoke that for some odd reason smelled vaguely of Louis XIII Cognac.

'I've gone over your prospectus,' he said. 'You're asking for a lot of money, Professor.'

'Every dime's accounted for, sir.'

'And what's my reward for giving you all these, ah . . . 'dimes'?'

Jack frowned. It wasn't something he'd

even thought about. 'Satisfaction?' he said. 'From helping architects — *deserving* architects — achieve their potential.'

'In other words, nothing meaningful.'

Jack's composure slipped a little, but remembering Jilly's advice he struggled to get it back. 'Mr. Harriwell, the young men and women who qualify for cash grants will be building the future. Isn't that meaningful enough?'

Harriwell unplugged the cigar and showed his expensive capped teeth in a cold smile. 'Not even close.'

There didn't seem to be much Jack could say to that, so he said nothing. But he could see this pitch going down the toilet, just like all the others before it, and his spirits began to sink.

Studying the tip of his cigar, Harriwell said: 'I know what you're thinking. You're thinking, *That miserable old sonofabitch, he's got all the money in the world so why won't he part with some of it to help others less fortunate?*, when you should be thinking: *How can I butter him up or change my prospectus so he'll give me my fifty million.*'

'Mr. Harriwell — '

'Forget it. I have home-field advantage. You play by my terms or you don't play at all.'

Jack was a breath away from telling him to shove it, but still he forced himself to hold his silence and listen.

Harriwell said: 'I own everything the architects design while I'm subsidizing them. I get twenty percent of their earnings for the first five years they're in the workplace. And the Foundation is named after me.' He saw the fires stoking in Jack's eyes and his smile broadened. 'Also,' he added, 'you have to take an anger-management course. I don't want any loose cannons representing me.'

Jack opened his mouth to speak, thought better of it and closed it again.

'Intimidated?' asked Harriwell.

'Disappointed,' Jack corrected. 'And maybe a little disgusted.'

'Oh dear. You're not going to cry, are you, Professor?'

Jack stood up fast and tucked his briefcase under his arm. 'Mr Harriwell,' he said in a low, anger-choked voice, 'with all due respect, you know what you can do with your terms.'

Harriwell cocked his head to one side, studying him now with something akin to pity. 'Now I know why everyone else turned you down. They saw you for what you are: a dreamer. Worse, a *righteous* dreamer.'

Jack somehow managed to smile. 'Better a dreamer than an extortionist, sir.' Turning, he walked back between the scattered chairs and tables, knowing that he'd blown it again, that Harriwell had helped him blow it by being so insufferably . . . insufferable.

Harriwell watched him leave, his expression faintly mocking. He puffed contentedly on his cigar for a moment longer, then grabbed the arms of the chair and pulled himself slowly to his feet. Collecting the cane he'd left in the corner, he went out onto the balcony that overlooked John Street, there to make a very important call.

★　★　★

Angry as much with himself as with Harriwell, Jack drove away from the

33

Maverick Club faster than he should have. To call the meeting a disaster was putting it mildly. He'd blown his last chance. And why? Because he was too high-minded to simply bite his tongue and do whatever he needed to do to get his hands on Harriwell's money.

After all, fifty million was fifty million, even to a multi-millionaire. Was it so unreasonable for Harriwell to expect a return on his investment?

He was so busy thinking about where it had all gone wrong that he didn't see the traffic light change to red until it was almost too late to stop. When he slammed on the brakes the Camaro's tires squealed, bringing him to the attention of a traffic cop parked at the intersection. He eyed Jack like a hawk, and when the lights turned to green Jack drove slowly across the intersection and out of sight, the very model of restraint.

In no mood to go back to the office and tell Jilly the bad news, he pointed the Camaro toward Jamestown Avenue and the *End Zone*, deciding to fortify himself with a couple of Coors first.

The *End Zone* was a shrine to the San Francisco 49ers. The original owner had opened the place within sight of Candlestick Park in 1961. Now the walls were one enormous collage of logos, alternate logos, script logos, helmet logos, groupshots of the various Super Bowl championship teams, shots of Kezar Stadium and The Stick itself, and portraits of just about every player who'd donned the famous gold helmet and red jersey, from Michael Crabtree and Ahmad Brooks to veterans like Jerry Rice, Joe Montana and John Brodie.

At this time of day there were only a handful of customers in attendance. Jack took a stool at the bar and ordered Coors Lite. Two stools away sat a burly man with a big, knocked-about face and strong-looking yellow teeth. Jack hadn't seen him around before, but he was evidently a hardcore baseball fan, judging by the San Francisco *Giants* cap perched on his head.

Will Brophy, who'd owned the *End Zone* since 1978, listened sympathetically to Jack's tale of woe while he rinsed and dried glasses behind the bar. 'So basically what Mr. Moneybags was saying,' he said when Jack had finished, 'is you can't win on the road, ergo your money tree has dried up?'

'Everybody fumbles once in a while,' Jack replied defensively.

'You didn't fumble, pal, you deliberately took yourself out of the game.'

'There *was* no game. Harriwell's terms were unreasonable.'

Brophy, a red-headed Irishman with a handlebar moustache, shook his head. 'Jack, Jack, Jack . . . it's all about *negotiation*. Didn't you learn *anything* from all those other meetings?'

'Some things you can't learn. Not if you still want to look at yourself in the mirror.'

Brophy snorted. 'There you go again: more of that tired integrity shit. Don't you know being noble went out with King-fucking-Arthur?'

'So I should've groveled?'

'Groveled, licked his boots, kissed his ass, whatever it took. Just so you got the money.'

'Now you tell me.'

Brophy sighed and turned to the burly man. 'Always the comedian, always the loser.' Then, to Jack: 'So what's next, Mr. Bridesmaid?'

'I'm cutting my sabbatical short and going back to Berkeley,' Jack said quietly.

'Headlines: Resident Genius returns, tail between his legs. See obituary.'

Another customer signaled for a refill and Brophy moved off to serve him, leaving Jack staring moodily into his beer. He'd come here for consolation, not criticism. But it burned because he knew Brophy was right. He *should* have locked his principles away and tried something he'd never tried before: played the game, done whatever it took to get Harriwell's fifty million and turn his dream into a reality. The ends more than justified the means.

But people didn't understand that his principles were persistent and had Houdini-like tendencies. No matter how well he'd locked them up, they would have somehow gotten free.

'For what it's worth, I would've told

the old bastard to go shove it, too.'

Jack came out of his reverie and realized that the burly man was staring at him. In his mid-forties, he had a deep, gravelly voice and a powerful body that was just starting to soften.

Jack grinned and raised his beer in toast. 'Thanks.'

They drank.

'Name's Frye,' said the burly man. 'Alec Frye.'

'Jack Monroe.'

'Let me buy you another one,' Frye said. He signaled to the bartender for refills before saying: 'I couldn't help overhearing. This Foundation of yours — it's non-profit?'

'Yeah. That's what Harriwell seemed to forget. He acted like he was buying a thousand shares of GTE.'

'And you — what do *you* get out of it?'

'A minimal salary. Period.'

'Then how come it means so much to you?'

'Long story.'

Frye grinned. 'That's what bars are for.'

There was no arguing with that, but it didn't make it any easier for Jack. He rarely talked about his Foundation; and even now, as he organized his thoughts, he felt his emotions stirring. 'It starts and ends with my Dad,' he said at last. 'He always wanted to be an architect. Had all the talent in the world, but he had to support his folks as well as mom and me and he ended up working double shifts on the docks.'

'I guess that makes him extra proud of *you*.'

'Maybe — if he'd lived. He died before I graduated. But the Foundation was his idea. He didn't want kids like himself to see their dreams go up in smoke . . . and that's why I *have* to make it work.'

'And this clown Harriwell — he was your last hope?'

'Unless you happen to have fifty mil' stashed away in your back pocket?'

He expected Frye to grin again. He wasn't prepared for long, serious, searching scrutiny to which the other man subjected him. Finally Frye said: 'Grab your drink. I think you and me should talk — in private.'

Frye's idea of private was one of the booths along the rear wall. When they were settled in it, Frye said: 'I used be a cop, Jack. Sergeant, Tenderloin district. And like most cops, I always needed more money than I could earn. So whenever the opportunity came along I did a little moonlighting. One day I met this guy who needed security for a shindig he was holding on his boat. I didn't do much, just made sure no one got tossed overboard or stole the artwork, but this guy, Brady Thornhill, was impressed. Said if I ever retired from the force, he'd find me a job.'

'So you're working for him now?'

'Was. For his wife, actually — Mallory. Combination chauffeur-bodyguard.'

'What happened?'

'I got tired of her breakin' my balls 'cause I wouldn't jump through hoops.'

'Been there, done that.'

'Ex-wife?'

'Almost-wife. Thank God.' Jack smiled. 'From bachelor degree to bachelor*hood*.'

'Score one for the good guys.'

They clinked bottles and drank.

Their friendship thus sealed, Frye went on: 'So what I'm thinking is this. You got a business plan? Some kind of proposal?'

'I've got a prospectus. It's in my car.'

'Okay. Maybe I can get Thornhill to take a look at it, meet with you.'

'You'd do that?'

'Why not?' He swigged his Bud, adding: 'But I got to warn you about one thing: If I can persuade Thornhill to meet you, look out for Mallory. She wants his billions for herself, so she'll do anything to stop him from funding you.'

'I'll remember that. And if by some freak chance this works out, maybe you'll work for me? Once I find the right building I'll need security.'

'Be my pleasure, Prof.'

They drank to that, and feeling a little more optimistic than when he'd first arrived, Jack finally decided to go back to the office and put Jilly out of her misery.

After he gave Frye a copy of his prospectus, he climbed into the Camaro and drove away. Frye kept smiling until the car disappeared around a corner.

41

Then his smile hardened and taking out his cell phone, he speed-dialed a number and said: 'He's hooked.'

For a moment there was silence at the other end of the line. Then a voice replied: 'Reel him in.'

5

When Jack got back to the office and told Jilly what had happened, her response was a predictable: 'How many beers have you had?'

'Not enough to invent a story like that,' he assured her.

'So let me just get this straight. You blew off one zillionaire and stumbled onto another all in the same morning?'

Mellowed by the beer, he deadpanned: 'I had to do something to save your job.'

He was cute when he was a little crocked. As far as Jilly was concerned, he was cute drunk, sober or anyplace in between. But cute wasn't going to help him achieve his ambition, and she wanted that more than anything. 'Jack, get serious, will you! One-liners might've bought you laughs on campus, but this is crunch time. We've reached rock-bottom. We strike out now and you can kiss the Foundation goodbye.'

'We're not gonna strike out,' he promised. 'Alec Frye's gonna come through. He has to. Dammit, he *has* to.'

★   ★   ★

He did.

A little after two o'clock he called to say that Brady Thornhill was throwing a party aboard his yacht, the *Star-Crossed*, that very afternoon, 'and he's agreed to give you five minutes to make your pitch. Interested?'

Jack felt a surge of electricity wash through him. 'Understatement.'

'All right. You know Belvedere Cove?'

'I know *of* it.'

'Then get your ass down to the San Francisco Yacht Club, like *now*.'

'Thanks, Al. I really don't know — '

'Don't thank me till it's in the bag,' Frye said, and hung up.

Belvedere Cove was an exclusive area situated on the south side of the Tiburon Peninsula, overlooking San Francisco Bay. By three o'clock Jack was tooling the Camaro along its narrow, leafy lanes, heading for the San Francisco Yacht Club.

Like the Maverick before it, the yacht club spoke of serious money. As Jack waited for the security guard to check his name against the Thornhill guest-list, he saw it in the long line of luxury yachts and sailboats that rocked gently in their slips.

At last he was allowed through the gates and found a space for the Camaro among all the Rolls-Royces, Bentleys and Mercedes. Much as he loved it, he had to admit that his car stood out like an errant brushstroke in a masterpiece.

Finally he went in search of the *Star-Crossed*. It wasn't hard to find. Occupying two slips facing the bay, it was smaller than some countries, but not by much. It was a long, sleek vessel with a large gallery at the bow that was enclosed by aerodynamically angled smoked glass windows, and three decks, arranged so as to descend toward the stern in tiers, until they reached a large swimming pool. The top deck, he noticed, also doubled as a helipad.

On the three descending decks, a

catered lunch was in full-swing, and a Pop band was switching effortlessly between romantic standards and soul to soft jazz.

Pausing at the foot of the gangway, he took a deep breath and muttered: 'I can do this . . . I can do this . . . '

But as he reached the top of the gangway a supermodel-type in a yellow and black jungle micro-bikini barred his way. The girl reminded him a lot of the Camaro, in that she was built for fun, too. She was tall and hard-bodied, tanned to a golden bronze, the skin itself covered by soft golden down. She was about twenty, with center-parted pale blonde hair that framed her high-cheek-boned face, large violet eyes, and a generous, full-lipped mouth that turned up at the corners.

Although she was slightly tipsy, she didn't appear to be having much fun. She held a champagne flute in each hand, and gulped down the contents of one before speaking.

'You must be lost.'

'Thornhill?' he replied.

'You've got the password. But you

don't look like you belong here.'

'Can I come aboard if I promise not to steal the Picassos?'

'Silly,' she said, screwing up her snub nose. 'I meant that as a compliment.'

'That's probably why it sailed over my head.'

'Stop it. You're making me feel good.'

She noted Jack's obvious embarrassment and said: 'You're thinking, *What could she possibly feel bad about?*, right?'

'It *did* cross my mind.'

'See, there's my problem. Everyone assumes that I live in paradise.'

He looked up at the gleaming white yacht. 'Don't you?'

'What they don't understand is, paradise is only paradise if you're happy living there. Otherwise it's the pits and — Oh God, I'm rambling, aren't I? Always happens when I drink champagne.' As if to prove it, she tossed the contents of the second flute down and then looked at him again as if she were seeing him for the first time. 'Who *are* you anyway?'

'The guy who walked Jill up the hill,' he said.

' . . . to fetch a pail of water. Oh yeah, I remember you. I'm going to like you, Jack.' She sized him up and made no secret about it. 'So you're the professor who hopes to con Dad out of fifty million dollars, huh?'

He studied her with new interest. So she was a Thornhill too. 'I see my fame has preceded me.'

She crooked a finger at him and he followed her up onto the deck. Everywhere he looked expensively-dressed guests stood gathered in groups, most of them forty and over. The constant babble of conversation was punctuated every so often by a burst of laughter or the clinking of glass against glass.

The bikini girl led him through the throng. When they saw her coming, the guests parted and acknowledged her with ingratiating deference. With Jack, it was a different story.

'Now I know how a goldfish feels,' he told the girl.

She grinned. 'Want to *really* knot their panties?'

Before he could reply, she stopped and

turned so that he ran straight into her. Immediately, she draped her bare arms about his shoulders and kissed him. Her tongue forced open his lips and probed his mouth. At the same time she reached behind her and unhooked her bikini top, so that when she finally stood back, the top clung to his chest and her breasts were exposed for all to see.

'Ooops!' she giggled.

Around them the guests gave a collective gasp. Equally surprised, Jack tried not to stare at her breasts, but they were so inviting it was impossible. The girl deliberately made sure everyone got an eyeful before she slowly retrieved her top and held the cups to her eyes so they looked like a bizarre pair of glasses.

'Where's *Lenscrafters* when you need 'em?' she asked.

It wasn't that funny, but the guests howled. Jack, aware that he'd started blushing, and concerned that this girl might cost him his last shot at obtaining funding for the Foundation, said sternly: 'All right. You proved your point. Game over.'

The girl quickly covered her breasts with the bikini top and then turned so Jack could hook her up.

'Don't you think it's about time you told me your name?' he said.

'Zella,' she said. 'Zella Thornhill.' Taking his hand, she led him down through the boat to the main stateroom. As they entered Jack had to resist the temptation to whistle. The phrase *no expense spared* had been coined for this room. It must have cost more than most houses. Concealed lighting showed him a state-of-the-art entertainment center, an enormous flat-screen TV, the latest CD and DVD systems, a high-speed internet connection. The furniture was mostly contemporary, designed by Tokujin Yoshioka, and the floor was covered in Nain rugs from Iran. But the room was dominated by an exclusive Parnian desk built from six different kinds of wood. There were mirrors everywhere, making the room look even larger; and where there weren't any mirrors there were paintings, both modern and desirable. Jack recognized a Calvetti, two Buscis, an Enrico Lombardi.

On the far side of the room, a tall, trim man of about fifty was regaling three gorgeous models who were hanging on his every word. Zella went over and tapped him on the shoulder to get his attention. When he turned and looked at her, she slipped her arm under Jack's and said: 'Dad, meet the Ph.D. I'm gonna marry.'

The room went quiet, which was exactly the reaction Zella had hoped for. The guests were not sure if she was serious, and looked to Brady Thornhill for guidance. The multi-billionaire looked at Jack, saw how uncomfortable he was and promptly grabbed his hand and pumped it hard.

'Congratulations!' he said, then hugged his daughter.

Zella pulled a face. 'Stinker,' she said, pulling away from him. 'At least you could have *pretended* to be surprised.' She stalked off.

Thornhill only chuckled, then turned back to Jack. 'You a Scotch man, Professor?'

'On occasion.'

'I got some fifty year-old Black Bottle in my cabin. Goes down smooth as mother's milk. Come on.'

Jack fell into step beside him and they made their way aft. Thornhill was handsome, with high cheekbones and a rugged jaw. He was deeply tanned and had penetrating hazel eyes. Beneath his Jay Kos suit he looked trim and fit. His once-black hair was just starting to gray.

As they entered the smaller, more functional cabin, Thornhill asked: 'Do you have any kids?'

'Uh-uh.'

'What do you think of my daughter?'

'I've only just met her.'

'Good answer. You know, a lot of folks think Zella's too wild, and keep telling me to rein her in. But all I see is her mother, just as pretty and high-spirited, and every day I thank God for giving her to me.'

'I can understand why, sir.'

'*Sir?* Hey, I'm not that much older than you, bub.' He laughed and poured whiskey. 'Alec Frye spoke highly of you,' he said. 'But recommendation from a friend is one thing. Business is another.

So I looked through your prospectus that much closer, and I have to tell you, I was pleasantly surprised.'

'Really?'

'Yeah, *really*. I'm a stickler for detail, but I can't fault how you've laid everything out . . . Makes damned good sense, too. What better way to protect America's future than by encouraging its potential geniuses — regardless of what field they're in?'

'I'm glad you feel that way.'

'I can't believe others haven't. Bunch of short-sighted morons . . . Of course I'll have to run everything by legal, but unless I've missed something, I — '

He broke off as the door opened and a tall woman entered, then stopped and looked from Thornhill to Jack. She was about fifteen years younger than Thornhill, with thick, coppery gold hair cut short, with a seemingly careless side-part and curly bangs. She was wearing a tailored black mini-dress that dipped between her breasts and showed her hourglass figure and long legs to great advantage.

'O-Oh, I'm sorry, darling. I didn't know you were with someone.'

Thornhill chuckled. 'It's all right, honey, come on in. I was about to go look for you anyway.'

'Uh-oh, did I overspend again?'

'Always. That's why I have deep pockets.' He indicated Jack. 'I wanted you two to meet. Professor Jack Monroe, say hello to the joy of my life, Mallory.'

Mallory Thornhill had pale, flawless skin that was agreeably freckled across her strong shoulders. Her eyebrows were thick and arched naturally over large green eyes, while a small, straight nose pointed toward a wide, confidently sensual mouth.

'Mr. Monroe,' she said as if the name were distasteful.

Remembering Alex Frye's warning, Jack nodded a wary greeting.

Mallory moved close to her husband and clung to his arm. 'A professor, eh? My goodness, Brady, are you trying to bring culture into our sordid lives?'

'It's about time, don't you think?' He winked at Jack over the rim of his glass.

'Be nice to her, pal. It's my money, but *she* controls the purse strings.'

'I wish,' she quipped. Then: 'You really must get back to the party, Brady.'

Jack dutifully took his cue. 'Yes, I've taken up enough of your time, Mr Thornhill. But . . . well, thank you. You won't regret this, I promise. I, uh, guess I'll wait to hear from you.'

'Don't rush away, Prof,' said Thornhill. 'Mingle. Enjoy.'

★   ★   ★

A few minutes later Thornhill entered Zella's stateroom without knocking, just as one of the crewmen finished bandaging her right hand. 'I just heard,' he said. 'Are you all right, princess?'

'Sure. Who needs ten fingers, anyway?'

'Be serious, will you? Does she need a doctor?' he asked the crewman.

Before he could reply Zella said: 'Be careful, Rick. Your job depends on the right answer.'

Rick said: 'She'll be fine, sir. It was a clean cut, but it won't need stitches.'

Zella's smile widened out. 'Good news, Rick. You just won me for the night.'

Clearly embarrassed, Rick glanced nervously at Thornhill.

Thornhill said: 'Give us a minute, will you?' He waited for the crewman to leave and then faced his daughter. 'What am I gonna do with you?'

'Make me happy?' she suggested.

'All right. Name it.'

'I suppose divorce is out of the question?'

His expression hardened. 'Is that what this is all about? Mallory? Is that why you — '

'Yes?'

He drew a breath. 'I spoke to some of our guests. They say that as soon as Mallory arrived your glass shattered in your hand and you cut yourself on the flute. Was it an accident or . . . ?'

'Why, Daddy,' Zella said innocently, 'what *are* you suggesting?'

'I'm suggesting that fifty-dollar champagne glasses don't just shatter when they think they will. I think you saw Mallory and . . . I don't know . . . I know she gets under your skin. I know you think she's a poor substitute for your mother. Zella?'

'What?'

He looked down at her, his expression serious. 'You're not . . . you know, going down that self-harming route again, are you?'

'No,' she said, refusing to meet his eyes. 'I don't know what happened. One minute I was just enjoying myself, the next, poof! The glass broke and I became one of the walking wounded.'

She could tell that he didn't believe that any more than she believed herself. She was the perfect cliché, the poor little rich kid, all alone in a crowded room. But he was right about one thing: Mallory's arrival *had* caused her to squeeze the champagne glass until it shattered.

Thornhill himself put it down to jealousy. Until Mallory came along, she'd had him all to herself. She'd seen Mallory as a rival for his affections, a gold-digger come to steal him away from her. Another cliché. But there was something more to it than that. Zella seemed to hate Mallory with a vengeance, and he had no idea why.

Calling the crewman back in, he said: 'If my daughter gives you any more trouble, Rick, you have my permission to paddle her butt.'

As the door closed behind her father, Zella turned her butt to the crewman and said: 'Well? What are you waiting for, Rick?'

★　★　★

Mingle and enjoy, he'd said. But Jack wasn't sure how it was possible to mingle and enjoy when he didn't really know anyone and everyone around him occupied a completely different social class. Still, he'd known better than to make excuses and together they'd all gone back to the stateroom, where Jack helped himself to a glass of *Clos du Mesnil* and a canapé and then found a corner to stand in. He figured he'd stay just long enough to be polite and then slip away and await a call from Thornhill's lawyers.

For the first time he realized that he'd actually done it: he'd found a backer for the Foundation. But the true significance of the moment had yet to hit home. It had been such a long haul, and yet in the end it had all come good within the space of one brief conversation.

He went out on deck and leaned on the rail. Although he'd presented a thorough case, there was still a lot to think about. They'd need premises from which to operate. They needed to get the word out there that the Foundation was coming and what it was going to do. There'd be staff to find, students to welcome, and with no precedent, they'd have to make it up as they went along. The thought scared him and thrilled him at the same time.

It occurred to him then that Jilly ought to share in his joy. He was about to call her when he realized someone had joined him at the rail beside him. He turned, expecting to see Zella. Instead he found himself looking into Mallory's cool, cat-like green eyes.

'Having fun, Professor?'

'In my own way. And please, call me Jack.'

'What do you think of the yacht — *Jack*?'

'Impressive.'

'It's named after me, you know.'

'I thought it was called *Star-Crossed*.'

'It is. But *Mallory* is from the French, and what it really means is 'ill-fated luck'. Brady didn't want to call his yacht *Doomed* or *Misfortune*, so he toned it down a little and called it *Star-Crossed* instead.'

'Good call.'

'More than you know.'

'Meaning?'

'Unfortunately, I *do* bring bad luck to others. Specifically money-grabbers.'

'I hope that doesn't include me.'

'Don't be modest, Professor. Fifty million puts you at the top of the list.'

Jack studied her for a long, worried moment, hoping that she was joking, but knowing deep down that she wasn't. He said quietly: 'I'm not a money-grabber, Mrs Thornhill.'

'I'm not saying you are,' she replied. 'I'm sure your Foundation is a wonderful cause. You'll just have to find yourself another pot of gold, that's all.'

The statement slapped him in the face and he knew a fleeting moment of unreality. Stupidly he thought, *What Thornhill giveth, Mallory taketh away*. But it wasn't funny, not at all.

'Enjoy the party,' she said sweetly: ' . . . Jack.'

She walked away, her stride confident, sexy and unstoppable. He watched her go, still numb, a part of him saying that, okay, maybe she was right to protect her husband against the money-grabbers, but he wasn't one of those. And she certainly didn't have to enjoy her work so much.

He didn't want to lose his temper but he did. In one brief moment he'd gone from winner back to loser. He drank the remains of the champagne and then threw the glass into the blue-green waters of the harbor.

6

Dejected, Jack descended the gangway, the sounds of laughter and gaiety coming from the yacht behind him only adding to his black mood. As he walked back to the Camaro, he tried to think of his next move — not that he had to think too long.

He drove away from Belvedere Cove, hooked up with Route 101 and followed it back across the Golden Gate Bridge until he reached a tree-lined residential street that dead-ended at the San Francisco Columbarium. He parked, walked through the gates and headed for the large, copper-domed structure that dominated the three acres of gardens.

Inside lay a miniature universe of inlaid marble floors, stained-glass windows, tiered circular balconies and impressive ceiling mosaics. The columbarium held the ashes of almost nine thousand people each presented in its own niche and its own particular and often unique container. But Jack was here to pay his respects to only one.

On the second floor he stopped at a glass-fronted niche behind which sat a brown-leather, lace-up football — the last resting place for his father's ashes. The plaque below the niche read:

JAKE E MONROE
1947–1992

He clasped his hands and bowed his head briefly. The mausoleum was cool and quiet, restored to its former neoclassical glory in 1979, following almost half a century of neglect. His father had always admired the building. It seemed a fitting resting-place for him.

After the heady atmosphere of Brady Thornhill's party, the peace was welcome and soothing. But try as he did, he couldn't shrug off his dark mood.

'Some kinda day, huh, Pop?' he said to the plaque. 'Reminds me of Little League ... always striking out with the bases loaded ... that look on your face

. . . Man, I must've been a big disappointment to you.' He choked up, and for several moments stared miserably at his shoes. Then he looked up and squared his shoulders. 'I'm sorry I failed you, Pop. But I guess you're used to that by now.'

Turning, he left the building.

When he got back to the Camaro, he called Alec Frye.

'Yo,' a voice answered.

'Al? It's me, Jack Monroe.'

'Jack! How'd it go?'

'It didn't.'

'Excuse me?'

'Oh, Thornhill was all for it, but — '

'Mallory nixed it, right?'

''Fraid so.'

'Tell me exactly what happened.'

'Thornhill thought it was a great idea. Mallory didn't. She didn't come right out and say I was on the scam, but that was her meaning.'

Frye was silent for a moment, then: 'Maybe if I gave Brady a jingle?'

'Nah. It wouldn't help. You were right; Mallory's got him by the short 'n' curlies. But thanks anyway.'

He ended the call, fired up the Camaro and headed for his office.

When he got there, he tried to hide how depressed he was. But Jilly knew him too well and said: 'I take it things didn't go according to plan?'

'Couldn't've gone worse.'

'So where does that leave us?'

'Looking for boxes,' he said.

'What?'

'I've exhausted every source of funding that I know of, Jilly. Thornhill was our last roll of the dice. All that's left now is to close up shop.'

'No way.' She wanted to hug him and tell him that everything would look better in the morning, but she wasn't sure how he'd take that. To her he was so much more than an employer, but to him she had never been anything more than an employee.

So she said: 'All right, so this Mallory woman turned you down. That doesn't mean you should throw in the towel. God, we've had turn-downs before. In fact, all we've *had* is turn-downs. You didn't quit then — '

'Ever heard that saying about the straw that broke the camel's back?'

'I've also heard that 'If at first you don't succeed . . . ''

'Yeah, well, I already have tried and tried again. And I'm sick of it. I'm also sick of trying to make ends meet for a dream that no one else believes in — '

If it's just a matter of keeping your dream afloat, I'm willing to give up my million-dollar-a-week salary.'

Her offer seemed to catch him off-guard. He looked at her as if he'd never really seen her before. There was something so intensely personal in the moment that she felt her throat tighten. Rising, he came and stood in front of her. They'd never been that close before, and Jilly felt exhilarated.

'You're a sweetheart,' he said quietly.

She thought, *Oh God, he's going to kiss me, he's finally going to kiss me.*

And he did.

A brotherly peck on the cheek.

'But you can only bang your head against a brick wall for so long,' he added. 'And I've had it, Jilly. Come Friday, I'm out of the Foundation business.'

She turned and went to the copy machine before he could see how disappointed she was.

Jack returned to his desk and sat slumped in the chair, doodling with a pencil as he tried to accept the fact that he had failed his father — again.

What was left of the afternoon waned and still he sat there, alternately going back over the prospectus and then losing himself in a world of his own.

Finally, Jilly said: 'Are you ever going home?'

He looked up and realized she was standing before him, purse in hand. He checked his watch and was surprised to find that it was five-thirty-five. Where the hell had the day gone?

'Look,' she continued when he made no reply, 'I hate to jump ship, but I've got to get over to my folks.'

'Go ahead.'

'Will you be okay?'

'Sure.'

'Well, if you need me . . . '

'No, no, see you tomorrow.'

He watched as she left and then wearily put his feet up on the desk. Outside, the sun was setting and the sky gradually changed colors. The traffic on 1-80 began to thin out. It grew quiet in the office, maybe too quiet, and he decided abruptly that it was no place to be right now. He was just about to get up when his gaze settled on the small, framed photograph of him and his dad occupying the corner of the desk. Jack was just a boy, seated proudly behind the wheel of the Camaro, and his dad, the car's original owner, was looking on.

Dad. Worn out and used up by the age of forty-five.

It hurt to look at him.

When he was a child, Jack had had no idea just how miserable and disappointing his father's life must have been. He'd been a bright, imaginative man full of ideas, but he'd quit school after the eleventh grade because the family needed money and they were hiring down at the docks. Jake Monroe had put his own life on hold so that he could do right by his family, and always promised himself that one day he'd finish his education. Only that 'one day' never came. Bills came. Kids came. And they had to be paid for.

Dad . . . he thought. *I wish things could have been different. I wish I could have made it* —

Headlights swept past the window, painting shadows across the office walls, and a few moments later someone knocked on the door.

'It's open.'

Alec Frye entered, squinting in the darkness. 'Thought I'd find you here, Jacko. Saw your Camaro parked outside.'

Jack got up and shook hands with Frye. 'Come on in and join the wake,' he said.

As Frye closed the door and turned on the lights, Jack went to the mini-fridge and took out two beers.

'I'm accepting condolence cards, if you've come to deliver one.'

'I'm hoping it won't come to that.'

'Oh?'

'I've got an idea,' the ex-cop continued. 'I'm not promising anything, but . . . do you have a tux?'

It was the last thing Jack had expected

to hear. 'A tux? No. Why?'

'Mallory's sponsoring the annual Policeman's Ball tonight and I think you should go.'

Jack laughed. 'Crash a party full of cops? Now that really *would* win her over.'

'For a start, you wouldn't be crashing it.'

'No?'

'No. I know the guy in charge of security. Once you're in, it's up to you.'

'Faint heart never won fair lady, is that it?'

Frye shrugged. 'What have you got to lose? You won't get anywhere just mooning around here in the dark.'

Jack considered it. Maybe Mallory *would* admire his persistence. Well, a man could hope. He looked across the desk at Frye and said: 'Drink up. We're going tuxedo shopping.'

★   ★   ★

'Know something, Blaine?' said Mallory Thornhill, savoring every word. 'Your balls are a constant source of pleasure to me.'

Blaine J Fallon, the Chief of Police, shrugged modestly. 'Well, after a while these things bring with them a certain . . . expectation. And I would really *hate* to disappoint.'

Mallory gave him a dazzling smile. 'It hasn't happened so far.'

'And I hope it never will. I'd hate to disappoint *you*, Mallory, most of all.'

They were dancing in the ballroom of the Palace Hotel, where the annual fundraiser was always held. Attendance was good. San Francisco's elite had turned out in force to support so worthy a cause. An enormous mirror ball turned slowly overhead, radiating multicolored pinpoints of light across the dancers, while on-stage a seven-piece band provided the music. White-jacketed waiters weaved between the tables around the dance floor, where still more representatives of the rich Nob Hill types socialized, the men in black tie, the women in expensive fashionable gowns and aglitter with jewels.

Standing just inside the doorway, Jack cleared his throat and fiddled self-consciously with his bow-tie. If he'd felt out of place aboard the *Star-Crossed*, he felt even more adrift here. But he was determined to go through with this. The Foundation was worth fighting for, and he couldn't honestly turn his back on it without know that he'd fought for it to the bitter end.

Fighting his nerves, he stepped onto the dance floor and dodged between twirling dancers until he finally reached Mallory and Fallon, then tapped the Chief of Police on the shoulder. As Fallon turned around Jack cut in and, smiling sweetly at the police chief, said: 'Excuse me if I make off with your partner.'

As he led her inexpertly across the floor, he smelled Mallory's perfume. It was intoxicating, like the woman herself. She wore a tight-fitting ball gown, red and strapless, with an intricate design made out of beads and sequins that plunged from her low neckline to her right hip. Her neck, wrists and fingers sparkled with diamonds.

He smiled at her, expecting her to be furious. Instead, he found her watching him with mocking amusement.

'Persistent, aren't you, Professor?'

'If the cause is right.'

'So you told me. But how far are you willing to go to achieve your ends?'

'Whatever it is,' Jack said, 'I'll do it. Short of incest and folk dancing, of course.'

She chuckled warmly. 'Ah,' she said. 'Oscar Wilde.'

'Actually, the jury's out on who said it first. Some people even credit it to W C Fields. But you get the idea.'

'Oh, I do indeed. You're game for pretty much anything.'

'Now you're twisting my words, Mrs Thornhill.'

'I can twist a whole lot more than that,' she said, and thrust her crotch forward hard against him.

Surprised, he felt himself stirring in his pants. She was a stunningly attractive woman and both knew he was aroused.

'Are you *really* willing to do anything to win me over?' she asked.

'Just about,' he said.

She smiled, a smile that he knew would be all too easy to fall for. But then something happened to her eyes; they seemed to sharpen and harden, and she said: 'Sorry. The answer's still no. Now, since I assume you gate-crashed this little shindig, will you leave quietly or do I ask security to throw you out?'

'Thanks,' Jack said, letting her go, 'I'll leave the same way I came. Under my own steam.'

'But not under any more illusions?'

He refused to play games with her. 'Goodnight, Mrs Thornhill. I'm sorry to have bothered you.'

He turned and walked off the dance floor.

Mallory headed in the other direction. Blaine Fallon tried to intercept her but she shook her head. 'Not now, Blaine.'

She went directly to the restroom, took her phone from her purse and called

74

a number. It was answered almost immediately.

'You were right,' she told the voice. 'He was crushed.'

'Good. That should soften him up nicely.'

7

Crushed was an understatement.

Numb with disappointment, Jack drove home, poured himself a stiff one and flopped on the bed. He spent the night dejectedly staring at the ceiling. The next day wasn't any better. He spent the morning in a kind of daze, regretting that he hadn't accepted defeat yesterday, as planned, but had allowed himself to be suckered into believing there was still a chance that his Foundation might get funded.

More by habit than anything else he went to the chess board and made his move: Queen's bishop to rook 3. Then he returned to his desk and sat there staring off into space.

Presently, Jilly got up and studied the board.

'Stumped?' he asked hopefully.

'Not in *this* lifetime,' she replied. 'There you go — king's pawn to king 4.'

It was a little before one o'clock and he and Jilly had spent a near-silent morning packing boxes and generally getting ready to close up, when the door swung open and Zella Thornhill swept in. She was wearing a fluorescent green dress that was so short it should have been called a T-shirt. It showed off her legs to great advantage, and if possible made them looked even longer and more slender than they already were. Indeed, the only imperfection in her was her hand, which was still bandaged.

She smiled, noticing the jealousy she saw in Jilly's expression; then she fixed Jack with her large violet eyes and said: 'So this is where you hang out?'

'Until the end of the week, sure.'

'Moving to a bigger office?'

'More like going back to teaching.'

Zella frowned and started to say something. Then, changing her mind, she smiled sweetly at Jilly. 'Hi. I'm Zella Thornhill. Okay if I borrow your boss for lunch?'

'Would it make any difference if I said no?'

Before Zella could reply, Jack said: 'I'm really not in the mood right now, Zella — '

'You'd prefer to sit around here, just waiting for the end?'

'When you put it that way,' Jack said. Then to Jilly: 'Call me if anything comes up.'

'You do the same,' she said cattily.

Outside, they climbed into Zella's scarlet 460 Spider Ferrari and roared off. Zella drove like Michael Schumacher, leaving Jack no option but to hang on for dear life.

'Before you ask me the obvious question,' she said, loudly enough to be heard over the Ferrari's powerful V8 engine, 'money can find anyone, and I've got the hots for you.'

He smiled sourly. 'I'm flattered.'

'Try terrified,' she suggested. 'And you should be. I'm a spoiled hottie who always gets her way and I have a mega-rich dad who'll personally kick your ass off the Golden Gate if you lay a finger on me.'

'And you're telling me all this fun stuff because . . . ?'

'I want to establish my claim before Mallory sinks her teeth into you.'

'You're too late,' he told her. 'She's already done that. Fatally.'

'I'm not talking about my dad's money or your Foundation — this is personal. I've got dibs on you. Just remember that when she tries to jump your bones.'

'Okay, enough,' he said suddenly. 'I like you, Zella, and I think in some weird way you believe you're helping me, but this conversation is *over*.'

She glanced at him. 'Am I embarrassing you?'

'No. Yes. And you're embarrassing yourself, too.'

She stamped on the brake and the Ferrari squealed to a halt. Behind her, the other traffic on Bryant either slammed on the brakes or swerved around them, the drivers honking angrily. Ignoring them, Zella waited for a break in the oncoming traffic, then U-turned and took him back to Stillman.

Hearing the Ferrari roar up, Jilly looked out the window and watched Jack say goodbye to Zella. She scooted back to her computer and pretended to be busy just seconds before he entered.

'That was quick,' she said.

'Ever feel like you've just jumped off a runaway train?'

'So being the envy of every stud alive didn't light your candle — that what you're telling me?'

'She's a knockout,' he said, 'and I'd kill to have that car, but — '

The phone rang.

Jilly answered it. 'Monroe Foundation. May I help you?' As she listened to the reply her eyebrows arched in surprise. 'I'm afraid he isn't here right now ... Yes, I'll have him call you right away.' Hanging up, she jotted down a number and handed it to him.

'Who was that?' he asked. 'And why'd you say I wasn't here?'

'I thought you'd like a moment to gather yourself before you spoke to her.'

'Her who?'

'Mallory Thornhill,' Jilly said.

★　★　★

The Thornhills lived in a Victorian palace on Pacific Heights, but when Jack called her back Mallory told him to meet her at an address in San Mateo. When he drove up, he discovered an exclusive Spanish-style condominium that overlooked the Coyote Point Country Park. Turning the Camaro over to the valet, he joined Mallory who was waiting for him outside the elegant entrance. She was a knockout in a brief, clinging pink shift that melted all of Jack's hostility. She greeted him with a slight knowing smile, adding to his uneasiness, and led him inside.

As they rode the elevator up to Mallory's penthouse, he felt her gently press against him. It was done so subtly that he couldn't be sure if she'd done it intentionally or accidentally.

The condo was spacious and functional. There were two bedrooms, a living room, a large kitchen and more besides. The place reeked of new money. But it also had a peculiar *emptiness* to it, as if it were seldom used.

Mallory pulled back a sliding glass door and led him out onto a wide balcony with a magnificent view of the eucalyptus trees in the park below. 'Sit down,' she said, gesturing to one of the scattered loungers. 'Martini?'

'Sure. Thanks.'

She fixed the drinks and handed him one. As he took it he said: 'Nice place you have here, Mrs. Thornhill.'

'Don't call me that,' she snapped, her relaxed mood suddenly evaporating. 'I may be Mrs. Thornhill everywhere else, but here I'm *me*. Mallory. There's a difference.'

'Sorry.'

She shrugged and seemed to relax. 'You weren't to know. This is my own personal slice of heaven, Professor Jack. The one place I can come to when I want to stop living in Brady's shadow and be my own person. He doesn't know about it and there's no reason why he ever should. Got that?'

'Got it,' he said. 'But why are you telling me all your secrets?'

She sipped her drink. 'Because I believe I can trust you. And I want you to trust *me*.'

'Oh?'

'Come with me.'

She led him back inside, across the travertine floors to the master bedroom. Halfway there he started to get an uneasy feeling, but told himself he had to be wrong about this. Who was he kidding, anyway? He wasn't seduction material, although she was clearly the seductive type.

He followed her into the master bedroom. Like everything else about the place, it was twice as big as it needed to be. There were two walk-in closets, an armoire wardrobe and an adjoining bathroom complete with sunken tub with gold-plated fixtures and recessed lighting. The bedroom walls and ceiling were mirrored, and statuettes depicting a wide variety of sexual positions had been placed everywhere. He was bombarded by images of himself — but more importantly, by images of Mallory. They enhanced her raw and undeniable sexuality, and held a bizarre fascination for him until he realized that her reflection had set her glass down and was clasping him around the neck.

She felt his muscles nervously tighten at her touch and frowning, she said: 'Oh God, you're not going to play hard to get, are you?'

'I . . . uhm . . . ' Jack hesitated, searching for a suitable answer, then said: 'In case it's slipped your mind, you're the wife of my potential benefactor.'

'All the more reason to keep me happy.'

'Mrs. Thornhill, please . . . '

Her expression hardened again, so fast and so completely that he stepped back from her. 'Jack,' she said softly, firmly, 'don't fuck with me. I 'come' with the money. No me, no Foundation.'

He heard the words but could not believe them. 'I never thought of it that way,' he finally managed to say.

'I know fifty million reasons why you should.'

She dropped to her knees in front of him and deftly unbuttoned his jeans. He wanted to tell her to stop, but another part of him, a stronger part, made him keep silent. His jaw tightened and his head tilted back until he was staring at his reflection in the mirrored ceiling. He didn't want to look at himself at that moment; neither did he want to think about the consequences.

'Make that fifty million and one,' said Mallory, her voice muffled.

Jack dropped his glass to the carpet and closed his eyes.

★ ★ ★

It wasn't sex, at least not in the way he'd ever known it. It was hard and violent, raw and uncompromising, and all four aspects were served to him in a way that was completely alien to him. But that's what made it so exciting. He really didn't relish screwing another man's wife, and he certainly didn't want to make his life any more complicated than it already was; but there was something primal about this woman, something free and wild and open. She lived for sex and knew no shame, and her outlook was contagious.

They fell back on the bed — the bed Brady Thornhill's money had paid for

— and she writhed beneath him, her legs encircling him, her arms coiling around his neck. Heat radiated from her. She seemed to secrete lust. She became a challenge to him, one he wanted to meet, a woman he knew he must never, ever disappoint.

He went wild with her.

Afterward, when they were wrapped in soft robes and sitting on the balcony again, she said: 'Do I scare you?'

He wanted to lie and say no, but he knew she'd see right through him. 'A little, I guess,' he admitted. Then, seeing her mocking smile: 'Okay, a lot.'

Mallory smiled, smugly pleased.

'What really scares me,' Jack continued, 'is how quickly I fell off my righteous pedestal. I've always bragged about how important it is to have values, and now look at me. Guess I never realized how precarious integrity was.'

'Does that mean you're sorry or glad?'

'That we made love? Jesus, that's a hell of a question. No, I'm definitely not sorry. Worried, maybe.'

'About Brady? Don't be. He'll never

know. And just to put your mind completely at ease, you're the first man I've ever invited here.'

Without thinking, he indicated his robe and joked: 'So this isn't one-size-fits-all, then?'

She threw her drink in his face, jumped up and stormed back inside.

Surprised by her sudden mood swing, he went after her. He found her hunched over the kitchen countertop, crying softly.

'Look, I'm sorry if I offended — '

She whirled around so fast that he flinched. But all she said was: 'Kiss me.'

Again he was caught off-guard.

'Kiss me, goddammit!'

He cupped her face in his hands and went to kiss her.

'No,' she said, panting. 'Lower.'

She opened her own robe, and he obediently dropped to his knees before her.

8

For one of the few times in his life Brady Thornhill was at peace with himself. He was wearing a skintight black latex mask and a body-hugging outfit of the same material, and he was facing a dull red wall from which hung a whole smorgasbord of sexual domination toys. His arms were raised, each of his wrists handcuffed to a large black hook.

Peace, yes.

As the dominatrix continued to paddle his bare red buttocks, Thornhill again found himself wondering what it was about pain that other people found so scary. Pain was a liberator. It gave the mind focus, perspective, made everything so much clearer to see. And it gave him the kind of hard-on normal sex couldn't, followed by an orgasm so powerful that afterward he felt completely drained.

He was reaching an orgasm now. He could feel it building in his loins, and he

Jack shrugged, the academic in him immediately surfacing. 'Anthropologists say it's a reminder of our prehistoric past.' He frowned. 'The first cave man, what do you think he was thinking as he gazed into the flames?'

'Hoping his wife didn't have a headache?'

'You don't think meat was on his mind?'

'That was on *her* mind.'

Jack chuckled.

'Because I like it,' she said as he studied her.

'W-What?'

'You were thinking, *Why does she always bring sex into everything?* Because I like it. Don't *you* like it?'

'Sure.'

'But not again? Not right now?'

He grinned sheepishly. 'Do you mind if we eat first? I've burned off an awful lot of calories today, you know.'

She laughed. 'Oh, I'm sure I can find something for you to nibble on . . . '

'There you go again.'

Rising, she vanished into the kitchen.

When she came back she was carrying a platter holding caviar, goat cheese and fancy crackers.

'You haven't asked me yet why I changed my mind,' she said as she settled back against him.

'I thought it was a woman's prerogative.'

Without warning she exploded. 'Fuck you!'

Jarred by her unpredictable temper, Jack felt his own anger flaring. 'Man, what is it with you Thornhill women? First Zella and now — '

She slapped him before he could finish the sentence.

'Don't you ever compare me to that conniving little bitch again!'

Cheek stinging, Jack said: 'Are we talking about the same Zella?'

Mallory sneered. 'Oh, she may seem adorable, but don't give her what she wants and you'd be safer with a fucking rattlesnake.'

'You serious?'

'It's hard to believe, I know. But I live with her, and she's hated me ever since I married her father.'

'Maybe she's trying to protect the memory of her mother.'

'I could excuse her if that were true. But according to Brady, Zella and her mom weren't close. She died when Zella was six. And that's her problem. She's had daddy all to herself for years and then, suddenly, I show up and steal some of his affection.'

Calming, she pressed against him.

Jack put his arm about her, feeling as he did like he was holding a grenade with the pin pulled.

'It's funny,' Mallory said, tracing a fingernail down his exposed chest. 'I can't visualize you doing stand-up.'

He frowned, puzzled. 'How'd you know about that? Been checking up on me?'

She didn't reply; just looked away uncomfortably.

'Brady?' Jack pressed. '*He's* been checking up on me?'

Still she didn't reply.

'If not Brady, then who?'

At last she looked at him, visibly ill-at-ease. 'Jack, I . . . I'm not comfortable telling

93

you this. She has enough problems without — '

'*She?*' And then: 'Zella? Zella's got me in her sights? Why, for chrissake?'

When she looked away again he grabbed her. 'Dammit, Mallory, if there's some kind of problem I need to know about it. *Now.*'

Mallory hesitated as if she did not want to continue the discussion.

'Please,' Jack said, 'I really need to know.'

'She fixates on people,' Mallory said at last. 'Men *and* women. Follows them everywhere, shows up in their beds, sends them nude photos of herself . . . '

'Jesus.'

'It's been an on-going problem and but for Brady's money, she would've been arrested more than once. Don't be too hard on her, Jack. It's not easy growing up as rich as she is.'

He nodded, though it was hard right then to imagine that having too much money could ever be a problem. Still, his opinion of Zella had taken a hit.

'Were you any good?' Mallory asked.

'As a comic, I mean?'

'One to ten? A four. But I managed to fool enough club owners to pay my way through Berkeley.'

'Let me be the judge of that.'

He thought quickly, then said: 'I tried sniffing Coke once, but the ice cubes kept getting stuck up my nose.'

'Ouch.'

'I know, I know. I'm depriving some poor village of its idiot, right?'

She sighed wistfully. 'I wanted to be an Olympic swimmer.'

'What happened?'

'I discovered boys.'

'And you've worn water-wings ever since, is that it?'

She sprang up suddenly. 'Come on,' she said. 'I'll show you.'

He followed her through the house until they came to her indoor lap pool. She stepped out of her robe and dove into the sparkling blue water, knifing through it as if it were her natural element. Jack watched her dart to the far end, surface, shake droplets from her hair and grin at him.

'I'm thinking those boys cost you a gold medal,' he said, skirting the pool to join her. His voice echoed off the vaulted ceiling and blue-tiled walls.

'It was worth it,' she smiled. She held out her hand and he grasped it, but before he could pull her up out of the water she jerked him in. As he hit the surface, she pulled him under.

His robe immediately absorbed water and made it twice as hard for him to push back to the surface. Not that Mallory was about to allow that, anyway. While he was still struggling she swam down beside him, used her legs to scissor-lock him and pull him down still farther, until his feet were touching bottom.

He struggled against her, lungs threatening to burst, and she responded by squeezing him tighter.

He looked at her, turbulent water bubbling up between them. Her expression was impossible to read.

Then he realized he could hold his breath no longer, and he thought: *She's going to kill me. She's actually going to kill me —*

96

But then, at the last moment, she released her hold and he kicked upward. He broke the surface, choking and spluttering, and looked around for her. She was treading water, watching him from about seven or eight feet away.

'Are you fucking *insane?*' he yelled. 'You stupid — you almost drowned me!'

Her smile was cool, pleased. 'But I *didn't.*'

Pissed, he climbed out, tore off the robe and threw it down. Then grabbing one of the nearby towels, he hurriedly dried himself off. All the time she watched him from where she was resting her elbows on the pool edge.

'Sorry,' she said without remorse. 'Sometimes I forget that other people can't swim like I can.'

'I can swim,' he snapped. 'I can swim just fine. It's breathing underwater I have trouble with!'

He wasn't trying to be funny, but it was amusing just the same. He saw her fighting not to laugh and after a moment he had to grin as well.

'Forgive me?' she asked.

Before he could reply, she climbed out of the pool, picked up a towel and handed it to him. Then she stood before him, naked, water dripping from the pink tips of her breasts, trickling down her hard, flat belly and slender legs.

'Please . . . ?'

Grudgingly, he started drying her. Even as he did he somehow knew they were going to get wet all over again, any moment now . . .

'If I tell you why I changed my mind, promise not to hate me?' she asked.

'I could never hate you. But you don't have to tell me if — '

'No, no, I do. If we're going to be partners we have to be honest with each other.'

He stopped toweling her and waited.

'It wasn't because I wanted to help a bunch of struggling architects. I changed it for purely selfish reasons: I need your help.'

He grinned mirthlessly. 'Sorry, I quit the bumping-off-husbands racket a couple of years ago.'

'Don't flatter yourself. I may not love Brady like he wants me to, but I do admire him. And I love what he gives me: a life of ultimate luxury.'

'Yet you're here with me,' he reminded her. 'Why?'

'I just told you: I need your help.'

'And screwing me was a step toward getting it?'

'Apples and oranges.'

'So what is it you want?'

'I want the Foundation named after me, and to be involved in its daily functions,' she said. Before he could respond, she added: 'Careful. It's never a good idea to bite the Golden Goose.'

'I'm not about to. But an explanation might help me understand you.'

'You'll never understand me, Jack. I'm not like any woman you've ever known.'

'I won't argue that.'

'I'm tired of living in the Great Man's shadow. I want the world to acknowledge that I'm not just a trophy wife. I've got ambitions of my own; big ambitions. I want to enter politics ... be the first female governor of California. Hey, if a fucking *bodybuilder* can do it, anyone can, right?'

'Good point.'

'Heading up this Foundation will launch me into the public arena as well as buy me a lot of favorable press. After that, who knows what doors will open?'

'Tomorrow the world, huh?'

'Don't be so cynical. It's what I want and what I'll get, with you or without you.'

'Then why bother with me at all? You could fund any important project and not have me as a thorn in your side.'

'Why do you have to be a thorn? Why can't you be my guiding light? I'll need one if I'm to become governor.'

'I'd love to be your guiding light. But my conscience may get in the way.'

'Conscience?' She grabbed him, tightened her grip on him and gently massaged him until he began to respond. 'Do you really think that's going to be a problem?' she mocked.

He didn't answer.

'Fifty-million-dollars, Jack,' she whispered seductively. 'The Foundation of your dreams. All within your grasp.' She rubbed him a little harder, staring him right in the eyes as she did so. 'Don't fuck it up,' she said.

His only reply was a low groan of pleasure.

★　★　★

It was dark when he left. As soon as the Camaro turned a corner and disappeared, a bulky figure in a *Giants* baseball cap, raincoat and jeans left the shadows across the street and headed for the condo.

The newcomer found Mallory stretched out on the bed, caressing herself. She looked at him with languid eyes and said: 'Poor baby, you're all wet . . . '

The newcomer started toward her, but Mallory raised her hand. 'Wait,' she said, as if training a dog. 'Say it first. Say, 'I love you Mallory'.'

The newcomer said: 'I love you, Mallory.'

She smiled, and finally beckoned her companion forward.

9

All next day Jack expected to hear from Mallory, but she didn't call. Then, late in the afternoon, he got a call from Brady Thornhill's secretary, asking him to be at Brady's office at ten the next morning. After he got off the phone he thought about what he and Mallory had done at her condo and wondered if word had somehow filtered back to Brady. The fact that he might be walking into a fire-storm did little to improve his mood.

He suffered through another anxiety dream that night, and woke well before dawn next morning. He felt steam-rolled. A shower and several cups of black coffee helped revive him, and he tried hard to remain upbeat until it was time to leave for the meeting with Brady.

It was ten o'clock when he arrived at Brady's headquarters — a thirty-eight floor office block on Market Street called Thornhill House. Brady's secretary, Alice, ushered Jack into her boss' penthouse office, where Brady was talking on the phone while riding a Lifecycle. He waved cordially to Jack and signaled for him to sit down. Jack obeyed, relieved to find Brady friendly but still puzzled as to why they were meeting.

Alice brought him coffee, then left them alone. Jack gazed out the wall-to-ceiling windows at the city and tried not to eavesdrop on the Thornhill's conversation. Brady's raised voice made it impossible.

'Congressman, I'd be happy to support you, but first you gotta make this 'underground river' shit go away. That hillside's in your district and we both know I can't build my condos until the geological report is signed . . . Yeah, yeah, I know it's an issue. But I didn't invest forty million to have some pissant geologist hold me up because he *thinks* the fucking hill might collapse . . . No, I don't care how you handle it. That's your problem. Just get it done and get it done fast or come election time, your opponent's war chest will be full of my fucking money. Get back to me on it, okay?'

He ended the call and got off the stationary bike. His FILA jogging suit was dark with sweat. As he grabbed a towel and wiped off the sweat, he shook his head at Jack. 'Dumb cocksucker,' he growled. 'Must think I was born yesterday.'

Jack got up and went to shake Brady's hand. 'If this is a bad time . . . '

'No, no, just a blip on the radar.' Brady crossed to a tray of cereals, fruit juices and vitamins. 'Juice?'

'No thanks.'

Brady helped himself to a glass of orange juice and then flopped down into the expensive chair behind an equally expensive desk that took up more space than most Haitian houses. 'Park it,' he said, indicating the chair opposite him. Then as Jack sat: 'I underestimated you, Professor.'

Jack felt his heartbeat quicken. 'Oh?'

'Anyone who can make my wife change her mind must know something I don't . . . ' He grinned and toasted Jack with his juice. 'You've got yourself a Foundation, pal.'

Happily shocked, Jack couldn't think of what to say. 'I have?' he said finally. 'I *have?* Hey, that's fantastic! Thank you, Mr Thornhill — '

'You earned it. Hell of a smart move, naming the Foundation after her. Playing on her ego . . . how could she refuse you after that?' He grinned again. 'Maybe you should come and work for me. You're smart, persistent, and God knows I could use someone I can trust.'

Trust. The word made Jack squirm.

'But first things first,' said Thornhill. 'You guys are gonna have your hands full hiring a staff, finding a building, ironing out all the legal shit — ' He paused briefly, then said: 'Which reminds me. I want everything to go through my legal department. I pay the fuckers millions of dollars for sitting around on their asses. It's time they earned their keep.'

The door clicked open and Thornhill's secretary entered. 'Your ten-fifteen's on line two, Mr. Thornhill.'

Brady nodded and said to Jack: 'I have to take this.'

'Thank you, sir. You won't regret it.'

'*You* will, if you keep calling me 'sir'.' He pumped Jack's hand, adding: 'And don't fuck my wife, okay?'

Jack froze, wondering for a moment if he'd heard Brady correctly. Deciding he had, he turned back to him. 'Mr. Thornhill,' he began.

But Brady was now on the phone, saying: 'You better have good news for me, Ed . . . '

Swallowing hard, Jack hurried out.

★　★　★

When he got back to his car he called Alec Frye and invited him to breakfast at Zackey's Coffee Shop, a location on Jerrold Avenue they both knew well. Thirty minutes later they were eating in a booth at the back of the diner.

'All I know is if you hadn't introduced me to Thornhill, I'd be teaching architecture at Berkeley right now.'

Frye shrugged, as if it was no big deal.

'Glad I could help. But the kudos are all yours. Getting that squirrely nympho to change her mind — how the hell did you do it, anyway?'

'I didn't. That's the weird part. She changed it herself. Wants to use the Foundation to leapfrog into politics.' He stopped as his cell phone buzzed. He checked the caller ID, then said: 'Hi.'

At the other end, Mallory said impatiently: 'Where are you?'

'Having breakfast. I was too nervous to eat earlier — '

'Well get your ass over here, Jack Monroe. I need to fuck you in the worst way.'

She hung up.

'Jesus . . . ' Jack said without realizing it.

'Problems?' Frye asked.

'W-What? Oh-h . . . no . . . '

'Look, I don't wanna poke my nose in where it don't belong — '

'You're not. It's just, I feel like I'm at a crossroads and don't know which way to . . . ' His voice trailed off and he was quiet for several moments. Then he said:

'Ever had to make the decision of your life?'

'Yeah, but it happened so fast it was over before I realized I'd made it,' Frye replied. He frowned, troubled. 'A druggie in the projects . . . wasn't old enough to shave . . . he pulled a gun . . . it was him or me . . . '

'But you did what you had to, right? And you survived . . . Dammit, so will I.'

Jack stood up and dug out his wallet. 'Gotta go,' he said. Leaving money for the check, he headed for the door.

Frye watched him go, thinking: *And so the dance begins . . .*

★ ★ ★

He was getting into his Camaro when Jilly called. 'Hey. What's up?'

'You've got mail,' she said. 'Specifically an email.'

'I'm sorry, is that so unusual?'

'It is when the sender prefers to remain anonymous.'

He settled himself behind the wheel. 'Well, what does it say? It's not trying to sell me Viagra, is it?'

'It says, 'Beware of Venus Flytraps. They eat more than flies'.'

'What's the return address?'

'Kinko's, on Van Ness.'

He knew it, vaguely. It was a popular internet cafe. 'So talk to the manager — '

'I'm way ahead of you,' she replied. 'Says he's been too busy to remember anyone specific.' She hesitated momentarily, then said: 'Any idea who it is or what they mean?'

'Not a clue. Must be a crank.'

'In San Francisco?! Well, I never.'

'Listen, I've gotta go.'

'Sure, sure. No rest for the wicked, yadda yadda.'

He ended the call, gunned the engine and headed for San Mateo.

★ ★ ★

After he left the coffee shop, Frye called Mallory. 'I don't know what you told Jack, but he's on the fence. Handle him with kid gloves or you may lose him.'

'Are you trying to tell me how to play a

man?' she asked.

'I'm telling you he's fighting his conscience,' Frye said. 'And right now, he could go either way.'

★ ★ ★

Jilly spent most of her lunchtimes at a gym on 3rd Street. Today was no different. Wearing shorts and a yellow tank-top, she headed to the row of Stairmasters. As she got close, she noticed Zella Thornhill working out on the end machine.

Jilly eyed her enviously. Zella was toned to perfection. Impulsively, Jilly stepped onto the Stairmaster beside her. 'Hi,' she said. 'I didn't know you worked out here.'

For a moment Zella couldn't place her. Then: 'Oh, hey! It's . . . ?'

'Jilly.'

'Jilly, right. No, I don't usually. But since I was in the area I thought I'd work off lunch.'

'Please, don't torture me,' said Jilly. 'I gain weight just dreaming about food. 'Course, it would help if I gave up *Ben* and *Jerry's*, but that's a sacrifice I can't seem to make.'

'Maybe you just need someone to encourage you?'

It was said so sincerely, Jilly gave Zella a second look. 'You mean like, go on *The Biggest Loser?*'

'Get out,' Zella laughed. 'You're not overweight. You just need some firming up.'

'You offering your services?'

Jilly was only kidding, but Zella replied seriously: 'I'd be glad to. But I should warn you: I can be a tough taskmaster . . .'

'Good. 'Cause I'm a lazy student. But what the hell, let's give it a whirl and see how it goes.'

'You're on,' Zella said.

★ ★ ★

As soon as he entered Mallory's condo, she was all over him. For a long time after that there was only sex, pure, animal sex, and the harder he treated her, the better she liked it.

Afterward they lay cuddled in the large round bed, Jack staring up at the mirrored ceiling, his mind elsewhere.

'Thinking about the Foundation?' she asked.

He nodded. 'And all the work that's ahead of us.'

'You'll handle it. I have faith in you.' She smiled at him, and he smiled back. But Mallory could never stray too far from her favorite subject. 'Do you mind me always being on top?' she asked suddenly.

'I hadn't really thought about it.'

'Don't you like to be on top?'

'I like it all ways.'

'Even with Zella?'

That made him raise up onto one elbow. 'What kind of cheap shot is that?'

She pushed him back down and straddled his chest so he couldn't move. 'She may be younger, and has those legs, but I'm the better fuck.'

'I really wouldn't know.'

'Uh-oh,' she said. 'Now I've pissed you off.'

'Damn right you have. I don't like being

made out to be the stud of the century.'

'Trust me, you're not.'

'To use your pet phrase, Mallory — fuck you.'

'You are so-oo cute. You can't even say *fuck* properly. You say it like the nuns used to — like saying it would break their hymen.'

'Jeeez-us — '

Mallory laughed. 'Have I offended you, Professor? Rocked your academic propriety? Well, I know how to fix that.'

'Don't,' he said.

She sat very still on top of him. 'What's wrong? If you're still pissed about that crack about you not being the stud of the century — '

'I'm not,' he said. 'I'm thinking about Brady.'

'Forget it. He wouldn't go for a threesome . . . '

'I didn't mean it like that. As I was leaving his office, he told me not to fuck you.'

'Brady said that?'

''And don't fuck my wife, okay?' His exact words.'

'Well, I wouldn't let it worry you. He's only joking.'

'I hope so,' he replied fervently. 'I really do, Mallory. Because what happens if he's *not?*'

10

Jilly was sorting through the mail next morning when she came to a pale pink envelope. She gave it an experimental sniff, then arched her brows.

'Whoever she is,' she said, 'she has expensive taste.'

Jack glanced up from the chess board. After much deliberation, he'd just pushed his queen's bishop pawn forward one space, to QB3. 'What're you talking about?'

'Chanel Number 5,' Jilly said. 'Three hundred bucks for a bottle the size of a postage stamp. Secretive too.'

'Huh?'

She turned the envelope over. 'No return address.'

'Let me see that.'

He snatched the envelope from her and opened it. It contained three postcard-size color shots of a naked girl. In one she was stretched out on her back with her legs spread wide. In the second she was on all fours, her right hand buried between her legs. In the third she was squeezing her own small breasts.

'Holy shit,' murmured Jack, realizing it was Zella. He looked up guiltily, as if he shouldn't have seen the photos, and quickly returned them to the envelope and locked it in his drawer. He'd destroy them later.

'Secret admirer?' Jilly said.

He reddened. 'No, uhm . . . I . . . it's junk mail.' He couldn't tell if she believed him, but at least she didn't pursue it.

The photos had rocked him and he had a hard time dismissing them — especially in view of what Mallory had told him about Zella. On impulse he Googled *Zella Thornhill*. There was plenty of material on her. There were photos of her attending society and yacht club functions, of her outside docks protesting against Japanese whale fishing and dolphin slaughtering . . . and an article headed

JUDGE THROWS OUT STALKING CASE AGAINST BRADY THORNHILL'S DAUGHTER.

The article read:

'Charges brought against Ms. Thornhill by Mr. Kevin Sykes were dismissed by Judge Figueroa for insufficient evidence . . . 'Right from the get-go this was nothing but a flagrant attempt to blackmail my client,' claimed her attorney, Mr. Cy Wald. 'If she wasn't the daughter of a billionaire Mr. Sykes would never have even considered going to court . . . ''

As soon as Jilly left for lunch, Jack called Alec Frye, ostensibly to see how security was coming along.

'Good,' Frye replied. 'I've got a shortlist of ex-cops who'll be perfect. Now all I need to know is when I can hire them.'

'Soon as I find the right building and see how much remodeling it'll need, I'll have a better idea.'

'Well, keep me posted.'

'I will. Uh, Al, before you go . . . do you remember a case against Zella Thornhill? Couple of years ago? Involved a guy named Sykes, who claimed she was stalking him?'

'Sure.'

'Was there any truth in it?' He listened to the uncomfortable silence at the other end of the line, then said: 'Just between you and me.'

'He had her dead to rights,' Frye said. 'But Brady's attorney bulldozed Sykes' El Cheapo shyster into submission. Why do you ask, anyway? She been hitting on you?'

'Uh-uh. Just making sure nothing can ever jump up and bite us once the Foundation's established.'

★　★　★

As soon as Jack hung up, Frye speed-dialed another number. 'You can rest easy,' he told Mallory. 'The photos drove him straight to *Google*.'

'I would've liked it better if she'd been found guilty.'

'Don't worry, Mrs. Thornhill. When I said Sykes had been railroaded Jack swallowed it hook, line and sinker.'

The line went dead.

* * *

After Jilly had gone home, Jack locked up and left by the rear entrance. Pausing by the dumpster, he struck a match and set fire to the pink envelope. He waited until it was nothing more than ashes and then got into his Camaro and drove to the *End Zone* to grab a bite. He sat at the bar, munching on a cheeseburger and fries and watching the news on CNN. During a commercial the bartender, Will Brophy, came up and said: 'Your buddy Alec was in earlier. Says you've finally hit paydirt. Congratulations.'

'Thanks,' Jack said. Then, his mind still on the photos, and why Zella had sent them to him in the first place, he added: 'Will, you meet a lot of women in here. Any of them ever stalk you?'

Brophy laughed. 'Never been that lucky.'

'I'm serious.'

'Okay. No. Why? Jilly stalking you?'

'Jilly? Christ, no. Why would you think that?'

'She was in here last week, tellin' one of

her buddies how much she liked you.'

'You're crazy. She's got a boyfriend.'

'That don't mean she doesn't want to upgrade.' Brophy walked off chuckling.

Jack finished his meal and headed home. But as soon as his brownstone came into sight he saw Zella standing outside. Parking behind her Ferrari, he got out and walked slowly up to her.

'Hi,' he said warily. 'What're you doing here?'

'Waiting to fetch our pail of water, what else?' When he didn't say anything, she added: 'You're supposed to say: 'The nursery rhyme's a crock, it's really vodka.' Then I say: 'I knew it. Who'd climb a hill just to get water?''

Again she waited. Again she was disappointed by his silence.

'What's wrong?' she asked finally. 'You off your feed?'

'Answer my question, Zella: what're you doing here?'

'Getting the cold shoulder,' she replied, all the humor vanishing from her expression. 'And I don't know why.'

He studied her, wondering if he should

say anything about the photos. But deciding it would only cause a scene, he said: 'I've got work to do.'

He went to brush past her, but she moved quickly to block his path. 'It's her, isn't it?' she said. 'My beloved stepmother. She's told you something that's turned you against me.'

'Zella, please, I don't want to get into this — '

'Don't I at least have the right to *defend* myself?'

'So I tell you and you deny it. What does that prove?'

'Since you've already judged me guilty, nothing!'

She stormed off to her Ferrari.

Feeling bad because she was right — he hadn't given her a chance — Jack hurried after her and grabbed her before she could get into the car.

'Zella, wait . . . hold it!'

She turned on him, tears of anger moistening her eyes. 'Why should I?'

''Cause I haven't eaten yet,' he lied. 'Have you?'

'No.'

'All right,' he said, his tone softening. 'Let's eat. And *talk*.'

★ ★ ★

They drove to Fisherman's Wharf. Here they bought plates of fresh seafood from a vendor and then ate on a bench facing Alcatraz and the few old Monterey Hull boats that were all that remained of a fishing fleet once numbered in the hundreds. The evening was cool and pleasant, the air filled with hungry swooping gulls.

Deciding she deserved to know the truth, Jack explained about the photographs.

Zella looked shocked. 'Jack, I swear to God I didn't send you any nude photographs.'

'Then who did? And before you say Mallory, answer me this: how did she get them and why the hell did you pose like that in the first place?'

Zella shrugged. 'I was probably rebelling against something that day or high or drunk . . . who knows? I'm not saying I've been an angel, but fixating on people . . . stalking them . . . sending them nude photos . . . no way.'

His silence told her he wasn't convinced.

'No matter what you've heard or read,' she insisted, 'it's not my style.'

'Okay, let's table that for a minute. You still haven't explained how Mallory got her hands on them.'

She looked away, and picked at her sea food.

'If you know something, Zella, now'd be the time to share it.'

'I don't. But my guess is she bought them off whoever took them. He was probably hoping to blackmail my Dad, like Sykes was, and somehow she got involved.'

'Why do I get the feeling you just made that up?'

'I know it's a stretch but . . . Oh God, Jack, can't you see what's going on here? Mallory wants you all to herself and she'll do anything to get you.'

'That's funny. She said the same thing about you.'

Frustrated, Zella glared at him. But controlling her volatile temper, she said: 'Okay, let's try something I've never tried before: let's be *logical* about this. What's my motive? We both know it isn't money. And though I admit you're cute, you're too old for me and — not to hurt your feelings or anything — not my type. And you can check that out with Dad. Soon as I'm hot for a guy he's on them like the FBI on a terrorist.'

He said nothing. But he was impressed by her apparent sincerity.

'So here's my deal,' she said. 'I won't bug you anymore, period. From now on, if you want to see me you'll have to call me. Then I'll come running. Cool?'

Without waiting for his answer, she got up, crossed to the railing and started throwing fries to the swooping gulls. He watched her for a moment. The sunset tinted one side of her silhouette. Then he set his plate down and pulled out his cell phone.

At the railing Zella stopped throwing fries to the gulls as her cell buzzed. Digging it out of her purse, she checked the caller ID. At once she turned and looked at Jack. Seeing him watching her with his phone to his ear cracked her up. She hurried over and sat beside him. 'Friends?'

'Friends,' he agreed.

'Cool.' She slipped her arm under his. 'By the way, I've been meaning to ask: did you pick your secretary because her name's Jill, or was that just a coincidence?'

'Jilly, not Jill,' he corrected. 'It's short for Jillian. And I didn't pick her. She picked me. A secretary wasn't in my budget.'

'But she kept coming back until she finally bullied you into it, yeah, she told me.'

'You've been talking to her?'

'Yeah, I ran into her at the gym. We have a lot in common, do you know that?'

'Sure. She was born in an Oakland trailer park with ten cents and you landed on Nob Hill with ten million.'

'Six hundred, actually.'

He whistled.

'Mom's family is even richer than Dad is,' Zella explained. 'And though I offered God a deal — all my millions if he'd give me back my mom — he wasn't feeling benevolent that day and said: 'Fuck off, kid, you're bothering me', so here I am, bothering *you* instead, and if you wanna know what Jilly and I have in common, we both wanna get into your pants, the only difference is she's too shy to tell you and . . . and . . . '

All at once she crashed emotionally, and whatever hurt and pain and misery she'd kept bottled up all this time suddenly hit her like a tsunami, and she started sobbing. Jack held her tight, allowing instinct to govern his actions, until eventually she stopped sobbing.

'Come on,' he said, helping her up, 'let's go home.'

She looked at him tearfully. 'Yours, I hope. Mine's more like a prison.'

'Mine,' he said.

★ ★ ★

Once in his apartment, Zella freshened up in the bathroom while Jack checked his emails.

'Feel better?' he asked when she

rejoined him in the living room.

'I'm not gonna cry again, if that's what you mean.' She flopped down on couch, adding: 'I could use a drink, though.'

He went to the refrigerator. 'All I have is cranberry juice and V8.'

'Yuk. What're you, some kind of health nut?'

'I eat out a lot,' he said lamely.

'How about wine?'

Jack shook his head.

'Well, I can see you're going to need some training.' She started to say something else then thought better of it.

'Go ahead,' he invited. 'There's nothing you could say that would shock me.'

She studied him, as if trying to get a read on him, then said softly: 'Tell my dad you've changed your mind.'

'About what?'

'Wanting him to finance your Foundation. Let *me* fund you instead.'

He laughed briefly. 'I was wrong. You *can* still shock me.'

'My money's as good as his,' Zella said. 'Plus, if you deal with me you won't have to — '

'Won't have to what?'

'You won't have to bang Mallory.'

He got up and stood over her. 'Out.'

'Do you deny you're banging her?'

'Out, out, out . . . '

He had to drag her to the door, and then push her out into the hallway.

'You're not the first, you know,' she said angrily. 'And you sure as shit won't be the last.'

'Zella, just go.'

'Don't you *see?* That's how she gets everything she wants. Check it out. Everywhere she's been she's screwed her way to the top. High school, college, Capitol Hill — '

He froze. 'Capitol Hill?'

'That's where she met my Dad. He was there with some lobbyists. Mallory was married to one of them but when she found out how rich and powerful dad was, she killed the guy and came to San Francisco.'

'Whoa, whoa. You're saying Mallory killed her husband?'

She shrugged. 'They said it was an accident.'

'Why is that so hard to believe?'

'Because. That's how she works. First she fucks you, then she kills you.'

He sighed wearily. 'Zella, enough, okay? Go home, will you? Please.'

'Sure, why not? I'm too late anyway. Even someone with your brains is no match for *her* magic pussy.'

11

'*You*'ve met Zella,' said Jack. 'Think she's capable of stalking someone?'

Surprised by the question, Jilly could only say: 'Are you nuts? Of course not!'

'I forgot. You'n she are gym buddies.'

'Hey, don't get pissy with me.'

'Sorry. I didn't mean to take it out on you ... It's just she's so damned unpredictable, I'm worried she'll do something screwy that'll make her dad change his mind and pull out.'

'Not a problem. While you were out his lawyers called. They want to know when you can meet with them. Sounded anxious to get the contracts signed.'

She expected his mood to brighten at the news, but it didn't. 'This Mallory,' she said gently, 'is she really as bad as Zella paints her? Or shouldn't I be asking?'

'Judge for yourself when you meet her.'

'Would that be before or after I buy my diamond tiara?'

'That reminds me. I meant to tell you — you're fired.'

'Wh-what?'

'I don't need two secretaries,' he explained.

'Jack, what the hell are you talking about?'

'But I *do* need an Administrative Assistant. 'Course, it means long hours, short lunches and a substantial raise — '

'I'll take it!' Jilly said. She crossed the room intending to hug him, only to hold back at the last moment. 'Do Administrative Assistants hug their bosses when they're happy?'

He grinned. 'Only when they're not genuflecting.'

'You've been watching too many porno movies.'

She playfully punched him in the stomach. Laughing, he grabbed her wrists and wouldn't let go. They wrestled around until she lost balance and would have fallen if he hadn't grasped her with both arms and pulled her against him.

They'd never been so close before, and the intimacy of the moment was electric for both.

They locked gazes. Neither spoke.

Then Jack kissed her, hard and full. Jilly responded passionately.

When they finally pulled apart, neither one knew for sure how best to handle it. Acknowledge it? Turn it into a joke? Pretend it hadn't happened?

They opted for the latter.

He cleared his throat and went to the water cooler. She returned to her desk.

Listen,' Jack said, 'Uhm . . . I'd better be, ah . . . '

' — going, right.'

'I mean, I don't want to be late.'

''Course not.'

'Okay, then . . . uhm . . . I'll see you later . . . '

'You bet.'

He got out of there fast.

★   ★   ★

Mallory was waiting for him when he arrived at Thornhill House. They entered the conference room together. A team of lawyers sat facing them. They rose when they saw Mallory and then one by one shook Jack's hand. Mallory took a seat at the head of the table, next to Jack. Then Thornhill's senior lawyer, Cy Wald, read through the financial agreement he'd drawn up, clause by clause. There were a lot of clauses.

Bored, Mallory pretended to be listening, but under the table she silently kicked off one shoe and with her toes began to rub Jack's calf.

Jack stiffened and felt his cheeks flush. Suddenly it felt very stuffy in the conference room and he found it difficult to concentrate on all the legal stuff.

'We almost done here?' Mallory asked suddenly.

'Close to it, Mrs. Thornhill.'

Wald finally handed her two copies of the document. She signed both and slid them to Jack. 'Are you coming?' she asked as he made to add his own signature.

Jack felt all eyes focused on him. 'Excuse me?'

'With me?' she continued innocently. 'Afterwards? To look at places for the Foundation?'

'O-Oh, yes — '

'What did you think I meant, Professor?'

Under the table her toes now climbed higher up his leg.

Jack began to sweat. 'Well, uhm . . . to be honest, Mrs. Thornhill, I'm not sure *what* I was thinking.'

He scribbled his name and passed the documents back to Wald, who gathered them together and said: 'Excellent! That's it! Once everything's been filed and we get your tax-exempt status approved by the I.R.S., you'll be up and running. Congratulations!'

Everyone shook hands and then the lawyers filed out. Mallory watched them leave, then stifling a yawn she stretched like a contented lioness.

Jack glared at her. 'Are you crazy? What if one of those clowns had seen you?'

She smiled wickedly. 'How do you know I wasn't doing it to them, too?'

That silenced him.

Mallory slipped her shoe back on and went to the door. 'Come on,' she said 'We've got premises to view.'

They spent the rest of the morning

being shown around a penthouse suite in Graham Towers. The walls were glass, floor to ceiling, and offered breathtaking views of the city. It smelled plush and new and full of potential.

'Well?' Mallory said at last. 'What do you think?'

'It's fabulous,' Jack said flatly.

'But you don't like it?'

Jack hesitated, then smiled at the realtor. 'Give us a minute, will you?'

'Of course.' The realtor left.

Jack turned to Mallory. 'Look, I meant what I said: this place *is* fabulous, and if we were lawyers or investment bankers trying to impress our clients, it'd be perfect.'

'But you have something else in mind?'

'Actually, I do.'

He called Jilly and asked her to meet them at the old Security Pacific Bank building. She got there first and was waiting when they arrived. The first meeting between she and Mallory was chilly but civil, and he realized that if these two were going to get along, they'd really have to work at it.

The Security Pacific Bank building was a 1930s-style brownstone just off Union Square, with a wedding cake facade topped off by two floors of old-fashioned offices. 'When Bank of America swallowed up the SPB, they sold the building off and it became home for half a dozen different businesses, all of which failed,' he explained to Mallory.

She surveyed the place with something less than enthusiasm. 'That augurs well,' she said coldly.

They went inside. The former bank was spacious and still filled with Gold Rush charm. It had high ceilings with decorative carving, the walls were covered in intricate murals and there were two old chandeliers in the lobby that needed repairing.

'The last owner turned the main floor into a restaurant that served tiny portions at exorbitant prices and went belly up before the paint was dry,' said Jilly.

'And you prefer this mausoleum to the penthouse at Graham Towers?' Mallory said to Jack.

'For our purposes, yes. It'll need

remodeling and the offices will have to be redecorated. But one of the suites on the second floor will make an ideal conference room. And the basement is perfect for a library.'

Sensing that Mallory was far from won over, Jilly added: 'Businesswise, it makes good sense, too. Instead of leasing offices and lining other people's pockets, the Foundation can buy the building and sit back and watch it jump in price.'

Mallory studied her coolly. 'What exactly is your job, Ms . . . ?'

'Ingram. Jillian Ingram, Mrs. Thornhill. As Jack just explained, I'm his Administrative Assistant.'

'How nice,' Mallory said. 'So I have you to thank for this . . . this . . . ' Unable to find the right words, she indicated their tawdry surroundings.

'No,' said Jack. 'Jilly merely reminded me about it. Architects use the past to help them shape the future. Being in an historic building like this will stir up their creative juices. Trust me.'

Once again Mallory gazed about her. Behind her back, Jilly crossed her fingers.

'How long will the remodeling take, and where will be working in the meantime?'

'Two-three months,' he said, adding: 'Graham Towers?'

'And you think the price is reasonable?'

'It's outrageous. But compared to what else is on the market, it's a bargain.'

Mallory shrugged. 'Buy it.'

Jack and Jilly exchanged smiles, barely able to control their excitement. Mallory caught the look between them and bristled.

'Let's go, Jack,' she said.

As she swept out, Jack glanced at Jilly. She nodded for him to go ahead.

Mallory waited until they were seated in the privacy of her limousine, then pinned Jack with a hard stare. 'You and this Ingram woman,' she said. 'Any shake 'n' bake going on?'

Jack frowned. 'No. Never. Why?'

'You do realize she's in love with you?'

'Mallory, for Pete's sake — '

'I'm a woman, Jack. Women know these things.' Before he could reply, she added: 'You should get rid of her.'

'*What?*'

'I won't insist on it — '

'That's generous of you.'

'For now, anyway,' she finished. 'But in time you'll see, she'll have to go. Now, let's move on to more *pleasant* things.' She went to slide her hand between his thighs, but Jack stopped her.

'Is this how it's gonna be, Mallory? First you kick my ass about something, then you pacify me with a blowjob?'

Mallory jerked away as if she'd been slapped. She pressed a button on the console beside her, said: 'Harris, stop the car. Professor Monroe is getting out.'

Jack gave her a disgusted look. 'My pleasure,' he said.

* * *

When he got back to the office Jilly looked up, surprised. 'That was quick,' she said. Then, catching his expression: 'Something wrong?'

Before he could reply his cell phone buzzed. He checked the readout. It was Brady Thornhill.

'Hello?'

Thornhill came right to the point. 'What's going on, Jack?'

Jack's throat dried up, but somehow he forced himself to say: 'With what, exactly?'

'I just got off the phone with Sid Levy in legal. He says there may be a glitch in the Foundation's tax-exempt status.'

Jack smiled sourly. *That didn't take her long*, he thought.

'Don't worry,' he said. 'It's just temporary.'

'I didn't get that impression from Sid.'

'He's a lawyer. They thrive on doom and gloom.'

'Amen. Well, if *you're* not worried *I'm* not worried. See ya.'

As Jack hung up, Jilly asked carefully: 'Speaking strictly as your Administrative Assistant, should I be worried?'

Jack laughed nastily. 'I'm beginning to think everyone should be worried.'

'What's that supposed to mean?'

'Forget it,' he said. With effort he shrugged off his dour mood and forced some brightness into his tone. 'Come on,

140

we've got work to do. Get me Joe McConnell over at Design Plus, and when I'm finished with him I'll need to talk to Doris Shaw at LDS International.'

12

When he got home that night and checked his mail, he found another distinctively pink envelope waiting for him. Just like the first, it smelled vaguely of Chanel Number 5. He opened it reluctantly and was more disappointed than surprised when he found another selection of photographs featuring Zella in poses which left little to the imagination.

'*Shit.*'

He burned the envelope and its contents over the sink, wondering as he did how it was possible for his life to have been so completely hijacked by the Thornhills. He then left the apartment and drove to Mallory's condo in San Mateo. The lights were on, but there was no response when he pushed the intercom buzzer. He tried again and this time kept his finger on the buzzer.

Finally, Mallory's voice answered. 'Yes?'

'It's me — Jack.'

'What do you want?'

'What do you think I want?'

'Forget it.' The intercom line went dead.

Frustrated, he buzzed again. No answer. He tried the door. It was locked. He hit all the buzzers. Finally a sleepy voice asked: 'Who is it?'

'Federal Express. I got a package.' The door buzzed and Jack pushed inside. Crossing the lobby, he rode the elevator up to the penthouse and banged on Mallory's door.

No answer. He banged again; harder.

Finally, Mallory opened the door. Her hair was messy and she was naked save for a Washington Redskins' jersey.

'I told you it was over,' she said coldly.

'What's over? What're you talking about?'

'Us. The Foundation. Everything.'

'You're pulling the plug because I won't fire *Jilly?*' he said incredulously. 'Jesus Christ, Mallory . . . are you crazy?' He angrily he pushed past her into the condo.

Mallory closed the door and leaned

back against it. 'Don't you see,' she said. 'This proves I'm right.'

Jack glared at her, so furious he didn't notice the *Giants* baseball cap lying on the coffee table. 'About what?'

'The Foundation's the most important thing in your life, but you're willing to blow it off to keep a secretary who supposedly means nothing to you.'

'It's called loyalty,' Jack said.

He went to the glass wall and stared out at the rain pelting down on the balcony and the park beyond, then turned back to her. 'While we're on the subject of 'blowing things off,' you once told me your dreams are linked to mine, yet here you are, letting a secretary 'sabotage' them.'

'And you aren't?'

'It's not the same. Jilly's the glue that held me together all these months. But for her support I would've given up the fight long ago. Firing her now would . . . Aw, hell,' he said, realizing he wasn't reaching her, 'maybe you're right. Maybe it just wasn't meant to be.'

He started to leave but she blocked his

path to the door. 'All right, you win. You can keep her. You can fuck her brains out for all I care.'

'And the tax-exempt glitch? Are you gonna wave your magic wand and make that disappear?'

She smiled the kind of smile that would have terrified any sane man. But right then, Jack wasn't sane.

'I'll make the call now, if you like.'

She went to the phone. He watched as she punched in a number. Then: 'Sid? Hi, it's Mallory. Sorry to bother you at this hour but it's important.'

The voice at the other end said: 'This is Alec, Mrs. Thornhill, not Sid.'

'Yes, I know,' Mallory said, adding: 'Sid, the problem you're having with our tax-exemption? Ignore it and go ahead with our plans.'

'Tax-exemption?' Frye repeated. 'I don't . . . ' Then the penny dropped. 'Oh, this is for Jack's benefit, right?'

'Yes. Will you take care of it for me?'

'Sure thing. Oh, and Mrs. Thornhill, is this to take precedence over that, uh, 'Ferrari problem'?'

'Absolutely,' she replied. 'That can be handled any time. Good night, Sid.'

★ ★ ★

She hung up and turned to Jack. 'Satisfied?'

There was nothing he could say but: 'Yes.'

13

Jilly's parents lived in a trailer park just outside Oakland. Her dad had once earned a good living assembling water filtration units at Brita and could have retired comfortably had it not been for the booze. But Eddie Ingram had always liked to drink; and after Jilly's kid brother, Dean, had been killed in an automobile accident, Eddie hit the bottle heavier than ever.

Dean's death had affected her mom, too. And though Jilly always nurtured a hope that she'd come out of it one day, she never had. That's why it had taken so long to diagnose her Alzheimer's. After Dean's death she'd grown remote, uncommunicative, preoccupied, and it had taken them a while to realize that her symptoms went deeper than just grief. It was only after she passed out one day and Jilly insisted on getting her checked out that the truth finally surfaced.

Late that evening Jilly parked her Chevy Aveo beside the trailer and let herself in. Even by trailer-trash standards, the place was a disgrace. It hadn't been cleaned or vacuumed for at least a month, and it smelled of stale booze and cigarettes. Nothing was ever put away, just left where it was. Her painfully-thin mother lay on a sagging couch, staring blankly at the nicotine-stained ceiling, her spittle-flecked lips working silently as she held a secret conversation with herself. Her father, at seventy-one almost ten years older than his wife, sat in front of the blocky TV, drinking cheap whiskey — a fat man in a stained undershirt and jogging pants.

Emotion made Jilly's eyes sting, but she knew that tears wouldn't make any difference to the way things had worked out for her folks. Nothing was ever really going to change their circumstances now, least of all her father. Eyeing the bottle in his lap, she said: 'That money I gave you was for groceries, not to buy you liquor.'

'I bought groceries,' he said without

turning to acknowledge her. 'They're in the cupboard. Take a look if you don't believe me.'

'I don't have to. I can guess what you bought. A box of macaroni and cheese and two cans of tuna. And I bet you needed someone to help you carry them to the car.'

He finally looked at her, bleary-eyed and belligerent. 'I'm doin' the best I can. If you'd do like I said and put ma in a home where she belongs, we'd all be better off.'

'I'm not putting mom in a state facility and I don't make enough yet to get her in a decent home,' Jilly said angrily. This was an old argument, and one she'd long-since grown tired of. 'But that's all gonna change now. I've been promoted and in a few days my raise will come through . . . '

He didn't answer but continued to stare fixedly at the TV.

Jilly sighed. 'Look, dad, I know this isn't easy on you. Or mom. But if you'll just hang on a little longer, everything will be fine. I promise.'

He didn't seem to care one way or the

other. Maybe he was past caring. He'd worked hard all his life, married, raised a family and hoped, if not expected, to enjoy his autumn years. Then fate stepped in: a sleep-deprived driver dozed off behind the wheel, his car killing the boy crossing the street in front of him. From then on nothing would ever be the same for the Ingrams again.

Jilly bit back her anger and gently kissed her father on the head. 'I'll let you know how it goes,' she said and left.

There were tears in her eyes as she got into her car. It had started drizzling and she looked back through the rain-streaked windshield at the trailer, just in case her father had bothered to get up and wave her off. He hadn't. She put the car into gear and drove away.

The two-lane highway beyond the park was undergoing repairs. Flashing caution lights illuminated a sign that said: *WARNING: OPEN TRENCH*. Parked off-road were several construction vehicles, already glistening from the shower, including a large, bright green asphalt distributor truck.

As she drove slowly toward the bottleneck, the lights of the huge truck suddenly flared over her. She squinted in the glare and saw the truck pull onto the street behind her.

Giving it little thought, Jilly concentrated on the street ahead, dropping speed still further because of the deep trench on her left. When she checked her mirrors again, the headlights were bigger, brighter. The driver was tailgating her.

The rain was falling harder now. Her wipers swept back and forth across the windshield, setting up an almost hypnotic rhythm.

A moment later the truck accelerated and rammed the rear of her car.

Startled by the jolt, Jilly cursed the driver and looked back.

The truck rammed her again, harder. Then again, only this time it maintained contact and started pushing her forward.

Alarmed, Jilly fought to control the wheel. At the same time she punched the gas, trying to drive away from the truck. But nothing happened except that the engine whined loudly and she realized her rear bumper must have snagged on the truck's front tow bar.

She kept honking the horn, hoping the truck driver would also realize they were hooked up and stop. Instead he went faster, the roar of his engine deafeningly loud. Jilly braked, hoping that resistance might make the driver behind her realize was what happening. It was a bad idea. He kept going, her locked tires smoking on the asphalt.

Then the front passenger-side tire blew and the car swerved violently toward the trench.

Panicked, Jilly desperately tried to straighten the car out. But the truck rammed her again and the car slewed off the blacktop and into the trench. It rolled over and over and finally hit the bottom. Jilly's airbag exploded in her face and everything went dark.

The truck braked above her. The driver climbed down. He was a burly man in a *Giants* baseball cap. He eased himself down into the trench until he was next to Jilly's mangled car. Seeing she was unconscious, he took out a pint of *Jack*

Daniels, broke the seal, took a swig, and then poured some of the whiskey on Jilly's lips. When he was finished, he dumped the bottle onto her lap and climbed back up to his truck.

He was a man who took pleasure in a job done well.

14

Jack and Mallory were enjoying the afterglow of sex when Jack's cell phone rang. He reached for it, checked the readout, frowned when he didn't recognize the number and said: 'Hello?' He listened for a moment, then: 'I'll be right there!'

He leapt out of bed and started dressing hurriedly. Mallory sat up, the sheet dropping from her high, hard breasts, and asked: 'What's wrong?'

'It's Jilly. She's had an accident.'

'*What?* Oh my God, is she all right?'

'She's alive. That's about all.' He grabbed his jacket. 'I'll call you when I know more.'

'Sure,' she said. 'Just go.'

He took 1-80 east across the Bay Bridge to the Alameda County Medical Center. When he announced himself at reception he learned two things: One was that Jilly had named him as her next of kin, which explained how they'd known to call him; the other was that she was in the ICU, and it was touch and go as to whether or not she'd even survive the night.

The bottom dropped out of Jack's universe, and when he went to ICU and looked in on her he was still numb inside.

Jilly was hooked up to a life support system, almost as pale as the pillow beneath her head. A mechanical ventilator was handling her breathing for her, a web of intravenous lines led to and from her body. Suction pumps, drains and catheters were working methodically to stabilize her condition, while yet more electrode-tipped wires were monitoring her bodily functions. To see her looking so still and helpless amid so much activity tore at his heart in a way he could never have imagined.

He shook his head and wondered why she'd named him as her next-of-kin and not her folks or her boyfriend. He tried to remember the boyfriend's name and realized Jilly had never told him.

There was nothing he could do, but he

didn't want to go home and spend the rest of the night waiting for a phone call. For *the* phone call. Glumly he found his way to the hospital waiting room. At that hour it was empty. A television played silently on the wall. He ignored it, sat down, thought about Jilly and couldn't believe that she'd driven under the influence.

Then again, what did he really know about *her*? She was always there, organizing his disorganized life as best she could and generally looking after him, but the nearest they ever really came to communicating was by chess, one move each day. He thought about her now, about what Mallory had told him about her being in love with him, and remembered the kiss they'd shared earlier on. He covered his face with his hands, realizing at last that she was more than just a secretary to him, more than the administration assistant, more than an opponent viewed across a chessboard, and he wondered why he'd never seen that before.

Because you've always been too wrapped

up in yourself, that's why. Because all that's ever meant anything to you is launching the Foundation.

The Foundation. Suddenly it didn't seem so important any more. In fact, it had ended up complicating his life in ways he could never have foreseen.

He picked up a dog-eared magazine, scanned one page and threw it back on the pile. Crossing his arms, he closed his eyes, thought about the past few days and wished he could go back and think everything through a little more carefully.

Somewhere along the way he dozed off. When he awoke forty minutes later he was no longer alone. Zella was sitting opposite him, watching him with a mixture of compassion and worry that he found startling.

'What are you doing here?' he asked.

'Mallory told Dad about Jilly. Dad told me. I had to be here.'

'You like her that much, huh?'

'If I could pick a sister, she'd be it.' Her face clouded. 'Dad called the CHP. They claim Jilly had been drinking and apparently lost control of her car.'

'No way.'

'That's what *I* said. But they found a bottle of Jack Daniels in her lap.'

'Impossible. Jilly never drinks hard liquor. Just wine and beer.'

A doctor appeared in the doorway. They both turned to her, half afraid, half hopeful. The doctor said: 'Professor Monroe?'

'That's me.'

'We've taken her off the critical list.'

Jack released a pent-up breath and felt lightheaded. ''Mean she's going to be all right?'

'Yes. She's taken a lot of punishment. Apart from all the superficial stuff — bruising, lacerations, concussion — she's suffered whiplash, she's got a dislocated ankle, two fractured ribs, a number of herniated discs, various ligament injuries and mild temporalmandibular joint injury. It'll be a long and painful haul before she's up and around again.'

Zella said: 'When can she be transferred?'

The doctor peered at her. 'To where, exactly?'

'The best hospital care money can buy,' Zella said.

★ ★ ★

Zella was like her father: she knew how to use the clout she had, and very quickly Jilly was transferred to California Pacific Medical Center, where work on her recovery really began.

As for Jack, the next few days were a blur. Remodeling on the old bank building had gotten underway. Restoration began on the original carving and pretty much everything else was torn down so that it could be quickly rebuilt.

One rainy morning he stopped by the office in Stillman Street to check the mail. It had piled up in his absence and as he started sorting through it he was reminded again just how much he owed to Jilly. He had no true grasp of what it took to keep the place running. Handling his finances, dealing with his correspondence, sending out invoices and settling bills . . . he found it all bewildering, and grew even more confused when he tried to use her computer to straighten everything out.

Time and again his eyes strayed to the corner filing cabinet and the chessboard with its game half-played. He told himself it was ridiculous how little things like that could come to mean so much, but they did.

He was trying to sort the mail into urgent and non-urgent piles when the door opened and a dark-haired woman in trendy glasses entered, her psychedelic umbrella still open. She closed it and shook off the rain. In doing so, she sent water in every direction, principally over all the rolled blueprints and scattered paperwork.

'Oh, shit,' she said. 'Sorry about that.'

Jack grabbed some paper towels and dried the blueprints. 'It's okay . . . '

The woman was tall and powerful-looking, with dark eyes, a long nose and a strong jaw. About thirty, she had broad shoulders beneath a short denim jacket, and wore tight black jeans that vanished into buckled Vagabond boots. Over one shoulder she carried a filled-to-bursting

160

Hello Kitty tote bag.

'May I help you?' he asked.

'I 'ope so. I'm Rosy Parker. I'm lookin' for Jilly Ingram.'

'Oh. She's not here. Is she a friend?'

'That depends,' the woman said dryly, 'on whether or not she gives me a job.' Then as Jack frowned, puzzled: 'You know. Secretary. You are advertisin' for a secretary, right? I rang her a few days ago and she told me to come in for an interview this mornin'.'

'Oh-h . . . now I get it,' Jack said, adding: 'You have qualifications, I take it?'

'Sure. Certificate in Professional PA an' Secretarial Skills. You want to see it?'

Jack shook his head. 'You know your way around a computer?'

''Course. I've got a Level 4 NVQ Diploma in Business an' Administration, too.'

He had no idea what that was, but it sounded impressive. 'Sit down,' he said. 'I think you might just be what I'm looking for.'

She gave him a questioning glance. 'No funny business, I 'ope.'

'Funny — ?' He broke off, then said: 'You're not from around here, are you, uh, Rosy?'

'England,' she replied. 'East London, actually. That's not a problem, is it?'

'Only if you don't have a Green card.'

'I do.'

'Then it's no problem at all. When can you start?'

'How soon do you want me?'

He looked at the paperwork scattered everywhere and made a decision. 'Take your coat off, Rosy. You try and make sense out of all this mail while I'll fix us some coffee.'

'Tea, if you've got it, Mr . . . uh . . . ?'

'Monroe,' he said. 'But I prefer Jack.'

'Jack,' she repeated, as if trying the name for size. 'Okay, come out the way and let the dog see the rabbit.'

Having no idea what she meant, he said: 'I'll go to the store and get some tea.'

'Earl Grey, if they've got it.'

'Okay. I'll pick up some Danish as well, just to celebrate.'

'Good idea,' Rosy said. 'I could murder a Chelsea bun right now.'

★ ★ ★

The old SPB building echoed with the noise of hammering, drilling and general demolition. Sometimes, as he tried to work, Jack was amazed that he could even hear himself think. But that was the least of his worries.

Shouting to be heard over the din, he pointed to the blueprints spread out across the drawing board and said: 'Bart, I told you not to eliminate those two chandeliers. Once they're repaired they'll add character to the lobby.'

Bart Sommers, the architect Mallory had brought in to oversee the redesign, gave a helpless shrug. 'Sorry, Jack. Mrs. Thornhill insisted. Said if you had any problem with her decision to take it up with her.'

'I will,' Jack said. His cell buzzed. 'Make it quick, Rosy. I'm in the middle of World War Three here.'

Rosy said: 'You received another one of those narky emails, Professor.'

He thought: *Great. That's just what I need right now*. 'What does it say?' he asked.

Rosy said: '"She's pulled the wings off one fly. You're next. I know. I love her too'.'

'Same return address?'

'No, this Kinko's is on Market Street.'

'And no one there remembers the sender?'

'Nope . . . But all this stuff about 'pulling wings off flies' sounds well out-of-order to me. Shouldn't we notify the Old Bill?'

'The who?'

'Sorry. The police.'

'No, they probably can't help. Anyway, I don't want any 'problems' connected to the Foundation. Just block the sender.'

'Already done it, Prof.' She'd tried calling him Jack but felt uncomfortable, so she'd decided to refer to him by his title.

'Thanks.'

'Oh, by the way — '

'Yes, Rosy?'

'Those undergraduates from Student Aid? They're about to pop in on you.'

'Why? They're researchers.'

'That's what I told Zella. But she insisted. Said it would give them a sense of 'istory — '

'Excuse me? *Zella?* What's she — ?'

He broke off as he saw Zella enter the building with a half-dozen undergraduates in tow. 'Never mind. I'll handle it.' He turned to Sommers. 'I want those chandeliers repaired and stored until we can hang them, okay?'

Sommers shrugged. 'Whatever you say.'

Jack hurried toward Zella and the undergraduates. Seeing his grim expression Zella told the students to stay where they were for a moment and then went forward to meet him.

'Hi, Prof,' she greeted. 'Rosy call you?'

'Zella, what the hell're you doing here?'

'Jilly asked me to help out — '

That stopped him in his tracks. 'She's conscious?'

'No. Before the accident. I would've checked with her again but since she can't talk yet, I — ' She broke off suddenly. 'Wait a minute!'

'What?'

'You still think I'm stalking you! Well, screw you, Jack Monroe! I don't need this shit.'

He grasped her arm before she could

165

storm off. 'Listen to me, goddammit. I don't think you're stalking me. I've had a lousy day, that's all. Mallory's fighting me at every turn and . . . ' He fell silent a moment, then said: 'Say it.'

'Say what?'

'Say: 'Jack does not think I'm stalking him'.'

'You're crazy.'

'Say it, goddammit!'

Grudgingly she said: 'Jack-does-not-think-I'm-stalking-him.'

'Now say it like you mean it.'

'Jack doesn't think I'm stalking him.'

'That's better. Friends again?'

'Always,' she said.

Jack's phone buzzed again and he swore. 'Told you, it's been one of those days.' Then he looked at the caller ID and quickly answered. 'Yes?' He caught Zella's eyes with his own. 'She *is?* That's wonderful, doc. Tell her I'll be right there.'

Zella's eyes went wide. 'Jilly?'

He nodded. 'She's awake. And she's asking for me.'

★ ★ ★

But if Jack expected some sort of miracle recovery, he was in for a disappointment. Although they'd taken her off life support, Jilly was still in bad shape. She looked pale, her bruises had turned sickly yellow, her eyes were dull, her lips almost colorless.

Holding a bunch of flowers Jack quietly entered the room and found Jilly dozing. He set the flowers down and gently kissed her forehead. She opened her eyes and managed a weak smile.

Pressing his hand over hers, he said: 'Hi.'

'Hi.'

'Now you can talk I suppose you'll want that raise?'

' . . . Ret-ro-active,' she said, her voice a faint whisper.

He had to swallow before he could talk. 'Naturally.'

She smiled again, and her eyes filled with tears as she looked up at him.

Embarrassed, he said, stupidly: 'How you feeling?'

' . . . Weak . . . '

'Well, there's a surprise. Guess car

accidents aren't what they used to be.'

That triggered something, and alarm suddenly entered her gaze.

'What's the matter? You okay?'

'It . . . wasn't an . . . accident . . . Jack . . .'

'What do you mean? CHP said — '

'Somebody . . . tried to . . . kill me.'

He looked at her, trying to decide if it was the medication talking or Jilly herself. She looked absolutely beat, but there was something in her eyes that was very much alive, sincere, terrified.

'Let me hear it,' he said gently. 'Let me hear it *all*.'

★   ★   ★

'A truck ran her off the road?'

Jack, sitting across from Mallory in her Graham Towers office, nodded and said: 'Then left her to die.'

'Jack, I know she's special to you but Brady says she'd been drinking.'

'He's wrong.'

'He heard it directly from the CHP.'

'I don't care if he heard it directly from God, it's still bullshit. I can't explain what

168

happened but I'm guessing whoever tried to kill her is responsible for the bottle as well.'

'But who'd want to kill her? And why?' Before he could reply she saw something in his eyes she didn't like. 'Wait. You think I had something to do with it? Fuck you, Jack.'

'I didn't say that.'

'You didn't have to! I can see it in your eyes. My God, just because you won't fire someone doesn't mean I call in my local mobster and have her whacked.' She narrowed her gaze at him. 'Do you *really* think I'm capable of murder, Jack?'

When he didn't reply, she said: 'Well kiss my ass and get the fuck out of my office.' Tears moistened her eyes as she glared at him. 'Check that — get out of my fucking *life!*'

'Mallory — '

'Don't *touch* me, you shithead!'

'Look, I'm sorry. Of course I don't think you could murder anyone. But everything's gotten so damned mixed up. I want you and can't have you. Your husband's financing my dream and I'm repaying him by — '

'Do you really?' she interrupted.

'What?'

'Want me?'

'You haven't figured that out yet?'

She sat back, suddenly drained. 'I didn't dare let myself. My life's been one disappointment after another. I've managed to survive them, but if I let myself think you want me and then lose you, God, that's one disappointment I don't think I could get over.'

Before he could answer, the intercom buzzed, breaking the moment and making Jack flinch. Brady's voice came through. 'Anyone there feel like lunch?'

It was on the tip of Mallory's tongue to refuse, but Jack shook his head. 'Sounds wonderful, darling.'

'Pick you up in ten.'

She switched the intercom off and turned to Jack. 'See you tonight? It's all right,' she said as he looked uneasy. 'I know you have to go see Jilly. But come to me after you leave the hospital.'

'I'll be there,' he promised. They kissed, long and hard, and then he went to the door. 'About Zella,' he said hesitantly. 'Any way you could be wrong about her?'

She looked pityingly at him, then took a Manila envelope from her desk drawer and threw it to him. He knew what he was going to see even before he pulled the photographs out.

'Where'd you get these?' he asked.

'From the man she was stalking. He threatened to sell them to the tabloids.'

'You paid him off?'

'Of course.'

'Why? These could've gotten her out of your hair.'

'Yeah, and broken Brady's heart. Thanks, but no thanks.'

He thrust the photos back into the envelope and handed it back to her.

'Sorry if I've ruined your 'bitch' image of me,' she said.

'You haven't.'

As soon as she was alone again she grabbed her cell and speed-dialed a number. When someone answered, she said venomously: 'She's running off at the mouth, you moron . . . How do I fucking know? Because she's already told Jack about your truck ramming her off the road! . . . Yeah. He was just in here accusing me of arranging it.'

'I'll handle it,' said the voice at the other end of the line.

'You'd better,' she said. 'And fucking quick.'

15

It was early evening, quitting time for the workmen involved in the renovation of the bank building but not for Jack himself. He was comparing blueprints to fix in his mind what had already been done and what was still left to do.

'She's getting there, Prof,' said Gary Baker, the foreman.

Jack looked around. 'But will I still be sane by the time it's finished?'

Baker grinned. 'That's remodeling for you. G'night.'

As Baker left, Alec Frye entered the building and hurried across the lobby. 'Hey, Jack.'

Jack turned to face him. 'Thanks for coming.'

'I work for you, remember? What's up?'

'Listen, Al, I know this isn't part of your job, but I need a favor.'

'Name it.'

'Look into Jilly's accident for me. The

CHP's blaming it on drunk-driving, but I know better. And Jilly swears that a truck rammed her off the road.'

Frye nodded, his expression giving nothing away. 'I'm on it.'

'Oh, and Al . . . ?'

'What?'

'One more question about Zella.' He hated to voice it, but it needed to be asked. 'Do you think she's capable of killing anyone?'

Frye considered that briefly, then said: 'That's the hell of it, Jack. We're *all* capable.'

★   ★   ★

When the doorbell rang, Mallory's whole mood changed. Jack was earlier than she'd expected, which meant he was eager. She hurried to the door, wearing only a man's shirt, unbuttoned. Out of habit she checked the peephole. When she saw the figure in the wet raincoat, gloves and *Giants* baseball cap, she stiffened and hesitated.

The doorbell chimed again. Reluctantly

she opened the door.

'I told you never to come here unless I invited you,' she said.

Her visitor said: 'But you don't invite me anymore.'

'I've been busy.'

'So I've noticed.'

Mallory frowned. 'You've been spying on me?'

'I wanted to know who'd taken my place.'

Mallory's temper flared. 'Don't you *ever* fucking spy on me again. You understand? *Ever!*'

She started to close the door, but the figure in the baseball cap stopped her. 'Please, don't shut me out. I love you more than anything. You *know* that. You once said you loved *me*.'

'I said I loved *fucking* you,' Mallory said cruelly. 'There's a difference.'

'I'll kill myself if I can't have you.'

'Don't be a drama queen.'

'I mean it. I'll kill myself. I swear I will. Then it'll all come out and you'll lose everything. You want that?'

She didn't, and her visitor knew it.

Grudgingly, Mallory stepped back and said: 'Okay, okay, come in.'

Her visitor went straight through to the bedroom, took off the cap, the raincoat, turned and allowed Mallory to feast on the near-naked body beneath.

Mallory grabbed her and began kissing her face, lips and throat. She then worked her way down, kissing the woman's breasts and belly, and finally the downy, musky shadows between her legs.

Zella's legs.

★　★　★

When they finished making love, Mallory said softly: 'Would you really tell Brady about us?' Then, knowing Zella so well: 'Of course you would. You're crazy enough.'

'Only when you shut me out of your life,' said Zella. She leaned over Mallory so that she could look straight down into her eyes. 'You don't realize what it does to me when you won't see me and I know you're in here with him.'

'What about Brady? Does it bother you when I'm with *him?*'

'Of course it does. But I love Dad and I get through it by telling myself you're making him happy.'

'And what about when I'm with you? Don't I make *you* happy?'

'Oh God, yes.'

'Then don't be greedy. I can't make everyone happy all the time.'

Rising, she picked up Zella's crumpled thong-panties.

Zella said: 'Where you going with those?'

'I'm throwing them in the wash. Borrow a pair of mine.'

She watched Mallory disappear into the bathroom and close the door behind her. Then she rose, entered one of the walk-in closets and helped herself to a pair of panties from a drawer. As she did so, her fingers touched something hard and cold beneath the jumbled underwear. Rummaging through it, she found a 9mm semi automatic. She frowned, surprised by her find.

She was just about to replace the gun

when she realized that it had been sitting on a sheet of white, apparently blank photographic paper. She glanced over her shoulder, heard Mallory showering. Quickly she helped herself to the sheet, turned it over — and froze.

It was a picture of Jilly getting into her car outside Jack's old office on Stillman. At the left edge of the photo, barely visible, was the center post of a sedan, indicating that the photo had been taken from inside a car.

Shaken, she replaced the photo, picked up the gun and like a pro pressed the magazine release button just behind the trigger guard. The magazine popped out of the butt and straight into her waiting palm. She checked it. It was full.

She frowned, troubled.

She replaced the mag, put the gun back exactly where she'd found it and then re-entered the bedroom, where she fished her cell from the raincoat and speed-dialed a number. Not once did she take her eyes from the bathroom door.

At last the call was answered. 'Hi,' she

said. 'It's me. Where are you?'

'In my car,' said Jack.

'You on your way to see Jilly or Mallory?' When he didn't reply immediately she said: 'Jack, don't play games with me. I know all about you two. About Mallory's secret condo.'

She heard him draw a breath. 'Zella, I'm sorry . . . '

'Forget it. Right now you have to go to the hospital and stay with Jilly until I get there.'

'Why, what's — ?'

'Just do it, Jack. It's important.'

He hesitated, trying to gauge what was behind the request, whether she was sincere or not. Finally he said: 'All right. I'm on my way.'

★　★　★

By the time Alec Frye pulled into the parking lot outside California Pacific Medical Center, the rain was finally starting to slacken. For a few moments after he turned off the engine he listened to its gentle drum on the roof of the car.

Then he took a pair of latex gloves from the glove compartment, pulled them on and from under his seat produced a small, zipped medical kit. He opened the kit, took out a syringe and carefully filled it from a vial of Aconitine, a poisonous alkaloid derived from a flowering plant belonging to the buttercup family. He stopped when he'd transferred a little more than a hundred milligrams into the barrel. That, he judged, should do the job to perfection.

Refusing to be hurried — even a single drop of Aconitine on unbroken skin could paralyze it for several hours — he replaced the cap on the needle and tucked it carefully into an inside pocket. Then he zipped the medical kit and slipped it back under the seat.

He looked through the rain-slick glass at the hospital. It was quiet now, after the daytime ebb and flow of patients and visitors. At last he got out of the car and headed for the rear entrance.

★ ★ ★

Mallory came out of the bathroom wrapped in a towel. She looked surprised when she saw Zella putting on her coat.

'You leaving?'

'Yeah. Dad's been on my case lately about rolling in too late.'

She went over and kissed Mallory.

'Love you,' she said.

She let herself out.

Mallory watched her go with an uneasy feeling in her stomach. After a moment she went back into the bathroom and fished Zella's panties out of the linen basket. She took them through to the kitchen, set them down on the counter, then opened the freezer and took out a small, wrapped freezer bag.

The bag unwrapped with an icy crackle. Inside, frozen hard, was a used condom.

Working with cool, clinical efficiency, Mallory opened the bag, tucked the panties inside with the condom and then held the resealed bag under the hot water faucet.

The condom did not take long to defrost.

Finally she shook the bag until she was sure that the semen had interacted with the material of the panties.

There was no going back now, even if she'd been so inclined.

16

Frye entered the hospital by way of a loading bay at the back of the building. It was too risky to use the front entrance. Even if he could get past the duty staff, his image was bound to be picked up by the security cameras there.

He made his way through the sleeping hospital, up darkened fire stairs and then out onto a wide, brightly-lit corridor. He looked both ways. The corridor was startlingly white beneath the harsh glare of the fluorescent light strips. He checked the nearest room number. By his reckoning, Jilly's room was five doors along on the right.

He was just about to head for it when he saw the door handle begin to turn from the inside. He hurried back to the fire stairs, where he waited with one ear pressed to the half-open door. He heard Jilly's room door close softly, then footsteps moving away, and when he chanced another look he was just in time to see a nurse vanish around the far corner.

When she was gone he stepped back into the corridor and made directly for Jilly's room.

Jilly was in a deep, drugged sleep. Good — she'd never know what hit her. Around her, an array of machines hummed softly as they monitored her condition. Closing the door softly behind him, he took the syringe from his pocket and pulled off the cap. He crossed to the IV tube and prepared to inject the contents of the syringe into it.

What happened after that wouldn't be pleasant. Breathing would become almost impossible. Jilly would begin to tingle and sweat, then turn cold and throw up. There'd be cramps and diarrhea, and finally cardiac arrest, and even if analysis of her blood or urine revealed the true cause of her symptoms, there was nothing anyone could do about it. Aconitine was a killer with no known antidote.

'See you, baby,' Frye whispered.

Behind him, the door opened.

Shoving the syringe back into his

pocket he turned quickly to find Jack standing there. Each man was as surprised as the other, but Jack found his voice first.

'A-Al! What're *you* doing here?'

Frye shrugged. 'Checking on how she's doing,' he replied smoothly. 'Poor kid, she's really banged up.'

Jack closed the door behind him. 'I didn't know you two knew each other.'

'Sure. I stopped by your office a few times, looking for you. Sweet gal.'

The conversation seemed to dry up then, and he gestured to the door. 'When she wakes up, tell her I was here.'

'Sure.'

He let himself out, and Jack went across and slumped into the visitor's chair.

★　★　★

Frye left by the main entrance and went directly to his car. He climbed inside and slammed the door angrily behind him. He didn't like failure and Mallory Thornhill liked it even less. Worse, she'd take her anger out on him.

He took out his cell and was about to call and give her the bad news when he heard a squeal of brakes in the distance. He instinctively slid down low so that he wouldn't be seen in the sudden glare of headlights as they swept the lot.

A scarlet Ferrari pulled up. Zella Thornhill jumped and ran into the hospital. Frye immediately called Mallory.

'Did you do it?' she asked.

'No.'

'Why not?'

'Because Monroe showed up, right out of the blue.'

'*What?* Did he see you?'

'Yeah. I said I was — '

'I don't care what you said. Did he say why he was there?'

'No. But Zella showed up a minute ago.'

'What's *she* doing there? Shit, now they're both probably talking to Jilly. I swear, Alec, sometimes I wonder what the *fuck* I'm paying you for.'

'Know somethin', Mallory?' he replied, his own temper flaring. 'So do I.'

In Jilly's room, Jack absorbed what Zella had just told him, then said: 'So Mallory's got a gun? What's the big deal? Lots of women own guns.'

'Not when they're supposedly scared to death of them.'

'You've lost me.'

'My dad loves to shoot skeet, right? He tried to get Mallory to go with him once but she begged off, saying guns terrified her.'

'Maybe she didn't want to go.'

'Then why not just say so? She's not shy about saying no. Anyway, she's told lots of other people how much she hates guns and wouldn't have one in the house. She's always going on about it.'

'Okay, for argument's sake, let's say you're right. She's lying. Why?'

Zella looked at the still-sleeping Jilly and gestured for Jack to join her outside.

In the corridor, she said: 'Along with the gun was a photo of Jilly getting into her car outside your old office on Stillman. It was taken from across the street. From inside somebody's car. You know. Like the person was spying on her.'

'Mallory?'

'Uh-uh. She wouldn't know which end of a camera to look through. But she's behind it.'

'Why is she spying on Jilly?'

'She's not; she's spying on *you*.'

'Me?'

'Why not? You're the one she's screwing. Sorry,' she said as he reacted. 'But it's the truth. She's got a lot invested in you. You're her passport to becoming governor.'

'How do you know about that?'

Zella hesitated. Then, deciding she had to tell him the truth, she said: 'She's banging me too, Jack.'

'*What?*'

He could see from her expression that she was serious. The idea left him shell-shocked. 'Just back up a minute,' he said. 'Let's take this one step at a time.'

He walked away from her, head down, thinking. She watched him get two sodas from the vending machine beside the nurse's station and then walk slowly back to her. He handed her a soda, then reached into his jacket pocket and took out the second pink envelope of photos, which he hadn't yet had a chance to destroy. 'What about the photos?' he said.

'Mallory must have a camera somewhere in her bedroom ceiling. I never knew it until you showed me those pictures she sent you.'

'That *she* sent me?'

'Well, who else could it have been? Bitch!'

He suddenly felt very tired and very, very unhappy with the direction his life had taken. 'Does your dad know?' he asked finally.

'You kidding? He'd kill me if he even suspected it. That's why all the cover-up . . . the fake horny routine . . . pretending I can't do without guys and sex. For his benefit.'

Jack started to say something then changed his mind. 'If you're wondering about Mallory,' Zella said, 'she has no preference.'

'Then she *is* sleeping with your dad?'

'Oh yeah. And from the sly remarks he makes now and then, she's doing more than spanking his monkey. But that's to be expected. When it comes to sex Mallory has no boundaries.'

He was silent. He could think of nothing to say.

'Look,' she said, 'I'm sorry to dump this on you, but — '

'How long?' he interrupted. 'You'n her?'

''Bout a year. I'd gone through a lot of emotional stuff ... flunked out of Stanford and was seeing a shrink ... life seemed pointless at the time. Then one night she came into this gay club I hung out at. We talked. I was lonely. She was so sweet and tender and ... so gorgeous. We went back to my place ... She made me feel special. Complete ... From then on I couldn't do without her and she knew it. That's her specialty, you know: getting her hooks into people then using them to get whatever it is she wants ... which in my case was my Dad.'

He sipped his soda without really tasting it.

'She really *is* a piece of work, you

know,' Zella said almost apologetically. 'And so am I for loving her.'

Both of them were silent for a moment.

'Think she could kill someone?' he asked then. 'Of course you do. You already think she killed her first husband.' He caught the unease in her expression and said sharply: 'What?' When she didn't answer, he lost his patience. 'Dammit, Zella, what?'

Reluctantly, she took an old newspaper clipping from her purse and handed it to him. He looked at the banner. It was from the *Traverse City Record-Eagle* and below the logo was a photo of an attractive girl identified as 20-year-old Marilyn Terrell, whose sister had drowned in Lower Herring Lake, Northern Michigan.

Marilyn Terrell bore a striking resemblance to Mallory.

'Where'd you get this?' Jack asked.

'From one of Mallory's photo albums. It fell out as I was looking through it. I never told her 'cause I was gonna show it to you.'

'Why didn't you?'

'What was the point? The coroner blamed the drowning on stomach cramps and I knew you'd only get pissed at me again for calling Mallory a murderer.'

He quickly read the article. 'Says she was sunbathing on a raft and didn't see her sister go under.'

'It also mentions she inherited their parents' house on the lake and some prime real estate in Traverse City.'

Worried about Jilly, he got up and tossed his soda can in the trash. 'Stay here, Zella. Don't leave Jilly alone for any reason. Okay?'

'Sure. Where you going?'

'To get her full-time protection,' he said.

17

But getting Jilly police protection wasn't going to be as easy as that.

At Park Station precinct, SFPD Lt. Warren Isaacs ushered Jack into his office, told him to sit and then returned to a mountain of paperwork. Finally, the tall, long-limbed black man looked up and said: 'I'm going to have to make this quick. I read the CHP report, Professor. There was no mention of any foul play.'

'What if I told you Ms. Ingram didn't drink hard liquor?'

'I'd find that hard to believe considering she smelled like an Irishman after a wake.'

'Have you checked with her folks?'

'About what?'

'To see if she was drinking with them? The accident occurred only a few blocks from the trailer park. It's hard to get bombed in a few minutes of driving.'

Isaacs said: 'Ms. Ingram leaves her parents sober; someone tries to kill her by ramming her from behind; then dumps whiskey over her to make it look as if she's been drinking? That's your scenario?'

'Is it so impossible?'

'Not impossible, just . . . unlikely.'

'What's so unlikely is that you think a woman I work with — a woman caring enough to spend most of her time and money supporting her folks — would suddenly turn whacko and invent a story about a mad trucker trying to kill her.'

'Look, Professor, I'd like to help you. But putting a man outside Ms. Ingram's door twenty-four-seven isn't in my budget right now. Besides, you've just said it yourself. A woman who's caring enough to spend most of her time and money supporting her folks . . . that can be a pretty thankless job even at the best of times. That's when some folks look around for a little comfort elsewhere.'

'Jilly isn't a drunk.'

Lt. Isaacs shrugged and went back to his paperwork. Jack realized there was little to be gained from arguing the point. 'May I use your phone?' he asked.

Isaacs pushed the phone toward him. Jack dialed, then said: 'Hi, Alice, this is Jack Monroe. Is he available? Sure. Thank you.' He waited a moment, then said: 'Brady? Hi. Listen, I'm sorry to bother you this late but I need your help . . . '

★   ★   ★

By the time he got back to the hospital a uniformed officer was standing guard at the door to Jilly's room, and Jilly was awake and wondering what was going on.

'Nothing,' he told her gently. 'Just concentrate on getting well, you hear me?'

'I . . . hear,' said Jilly. Her voice was a low, exhausted rasp. 'Thanks, Jack.'

'What for?'

'For caring,' she said. 'For *believing*.'

'Listen, I have to go. But Zella's gonna stay and keep you company.'

'Sorry I'm . . . such a pain . . . '

'Don't worry,' he deadpanned. 'I'm deducting it from your salary.'

She managed a weak smile.

'By the way,' he added, 'Queen's bishop pawn to QB3. Get out of that.'

He kissed her gently on the forehead and winked at Zella. As he closed the door behind him, Zella squeezed Jilly's hand. 'Get some zees,' she advised. 'I need my workout buddy back.'

Jilly nodded, closed her eyes and drifted off.

★　★　★

Jack drove out to San Mateo, where Mallory met him at the door of her condo with a martini in hand.

'You look like you could use this,' she said.

'This and three more like it.'

He let her lead him to the couch. Once he was seated, she draped herself across him and stroked his hair. 'How's Jilly?' she asked.

'Hanging in there.'

'Thank God.' She kissed him, and though he didn't resist she quickly noticed that he didn't respond, either. 'What you need, Professor, is some of Dr.

Mallory's special T.L.C.'

She went to unzip his fly but he stopped her.

'I hope this isn't a trend,' she said, hurt by the rejection. 'Anything else I can do for you?' When he shook his head, she said: 'I'm confused.'

'About why I came here, you mean? I'm not sure myself.' He finished his drink, stood up and frowned at her.

'I feel another accusation coming on,' she said.

'I was just wondering how you knew where I lived. Did Brady tell you?'

'He might've. I don't remember. Why, are you inviting me over?'

For a moment he was tempted to have it out with her, but he knew that he'd lose the Foundation if he did.

'Goodnight,' he said. He left.

★   ★   ★

When Mallory came through the door of the family home in Pacific Heights, she found Zella waiting for her in the vast, tiled lobby.

'Have fun tonight?' Zella asked.

Mallory wasn't in the mood for her. 'Get out of my way,' she warned.

But Zella didn't move. 'Don't be so unsociable — *mother*.'

'All right,' Mallory said wearily. 'What the fuck do you want?'

'I want you to leave Jack and Jilly alone. If anything happens to either one of them, I'll tell Dad everything.'

'Sure you will.'

Again she tried to go around Zella. Again Zella held her ground. 'Just so you know I'm serious — much as I love you, I won't let you hurt them. And to prove I mean it, I've already told Jack about us.'

Mallory flinched.

'Hit a nerve, did I?' asked Zella. Without waiting for a reply, she turned and headed for one of the two sweeping staircases that led up to the wide central gallery. 'Telling Dad?' she added. 'That'll almost be a relief. Sweet dreams.'

She reached the top of the stairs, then turned and looked down at Mallory.

'Oh, and those photos you sent Jack? I hope you have copies, 'cause they're the last ones you'll ever take of me.'

Mallory watched her disappear from view, listened to her heels on the expensive flooring, finally heard Zella's bedroom door slam shut. Barely able to contain her anger, she took out her cell and dialed. When she spoke, it was between her clenched teeth: 'Tomorrow morning. Usual time.'

★ ★ ★

Early the next morning Mallory's Bentley pulled up near the Conservatory of Flowers. Frye came up just as the rear window lowered. Mallory, wearing dark glasses, handed him an envelope. Frye took it, glanced inside, and frowned.

'This isn't what we agreed on.'

'You'll get the other half when you do the job. This time, no fuck-ups.'

The tinted window raised, hiding her from Frye. A moment later the Bentley drove smoothly away.

Frye watched it go, tight-lipped and enigmatic. Then he slowly smiled.

For Jack, the next few days were a blur.
But by the end of the week, he finally
allowed himself to believe that they were
actually making headway. On a bright
Monday morning he and Mallory showed
Brady around, and he liked what he saw.
The lobby now possessed a grandeur that
chrome, steel and glass could never hope
to match. Workmen were setting up
drafting tables by the windows, while
painters on scaffolding added the final
touches to walls and ceiling.

'Hell of a job, Jacko,' Brady said at the
end of the tour.

'Thanks. All that's left now is to
interview the architects we think deserve
cash grants, and we're starting that
tomorrow morning.'

Brady nodded. 'I've been thinking.
How about we throw a 'Grand Opening'
bash at the Fairmont? That ought to buy
us some valuable publicity.'

Mallory almost purred. 'It'll also give
me a chance to show off my new emerald
necklace.' She reached up and pecked

Thornhill on the cheek. 'Thank you for being so understanding.'

'It's only money, baby,' said Thornhill. 'And I'd rather give it to you than the government.' He glanced up at the clock. It was almost ten. 'Listen, I gotta run.'

He grabbed Jack's hand and pumped it enthusiastically. 'I'm proud of you, Jack. You too, baby.'

He kissed Mallory and hurried out. She smiled at Jack. 'How's it feel to achieve your dream?'

'It hasn't sunk in yet. But I'm sure when it does . . . ' His voice trailed off and he looked wistfully about him.

'Wishing your dad was here?' she guessed.

Jack grinned. 'I guess Old Man Harriwell was right: my face *is* an open book.'

'See you back at the office,' she told him. 'Have fun.'

He watched her leave, then gazed around proudly. *What do you think, Pop?* he wondered. *Did I finally hit one out of the park?*

★ ★ ★

Zella followed the jogging path down to the water's edge. There she stopped and stood for a while with hands on hips, looking out at the Golden Gate Bridge, silhouetted against the fierce red-orange of the dawn sky. She was breathing hard and her tank-top and shorts were soaked with sweat, but she felt good, alive.

The past couple of weeks had been the best ever. Confessing her secret to Jack was the best thing she could have done. It had been like having a weight lifted off her back and for the first time that she could remember she felt able to move forward with her life.

Jilly had unknowingly played her part, too. Zella had spent whole days with her, helping her to recover both physically and mentally from the accident, and that had been a new emotion for Zella, too — a feeling of reward; knowing that for the first time she was actually getting satisfaction from doing something for someone else.

She headed for her Ferrari. It was

parked about fifty yards away, by the guard-rail on a rocky point overlooking the Bay. On reaching it, she took out a towel and quickly wiped away the sweat, then climbed in behind the wheel.

That's when it happened.

She heard the growl of its 650-hp engine first, and then the massive red-and-white Mack Titan came roaring across the otherwise empty lot, its big chrome grille aimed right at her. She had one brief moment to look at the huge truck bearing down on her, and then —

Zella reached for the door handle, knowing even as she did so that she was going to be too late, because her fate had already been decided for her.

The Titan hit the back of the Ferrari, crunching it and ramming the car into the guard-rail. The guard-rail twisted and came loose, and the front wheels of the car rolled forward and dropped over the edge.

One more push finished the job.

The Ferrari teetered for a moment . . . then it plunged over the lip and into the water below.

In the cab of the heavy truck Alec Frye set the hand-brake and let the engine idle as he called Mallory on his cell and told her it was over.

'You're sure this time?' she said. 'I mean absolutely? No slip-ups?'

'None. By now, what the sharks haven't eaten is being swept out to sea.'

18

Brady Thornhill watched the tow-truck crane haul the mangled Ferrari out of the water. A crumpled section of guard-rail still clung to its bumper. Police had taped off the area, keeping the growing crowd back. Squad cars, paramedics, the media — the place was a madhouse.

Thornhill and Lieutenant Isaacs stood at the edge of the lot, watching as two police divers surfaced and then gestured that they hadn't found anything else — yet.

'Tell 'em to keep searching,' Thornhill said, lifelessly.

'But, sir, the tide — '

'*Do it, dammit!*'

Isaacs signaled for the divers to keep at it.

Mallory's Bentley raced up. Jumping out she pushed through the crowd to the tape. A police officer quickly intercepted her, then allowed her to pass when she told him who she was. She ran to Brady, hugged him and then broke down. Brady, tearful himself, did his best to stay strong.

★ ★ ★

Jack took it hard.

Jilly took it harder still.

'She *c-can't* be dead . . . She can't be! Jack, we had so many fun things planned. She even bought me a BMW.'

'A Bimmer?' he said, surprised.

'Oh, I wasn't gonna keep it, but . . . ' Her voice broke and she couldn't continue.

He reached for her and, mindful of her injuries, gently hugged her. 'Let it out,' he whispered. 'Let it all out, baby . . . '

He stared out the window as she wept. He couldn't believe he'd never see Zella again. She'd always been so vital . . . But at the same time it was impossible not to draw a comparison with what had happened to Jilly. One car rammed into a ditch, the other rammed into the Pacific. The police surely would see the similarity, the connection, and now take what had happened to Jilly more seriously.

Ever since he'd hooked up with the Thornhills things had gone from bad to worse. Oh, he'd gotten his money for the Foundation, but at what price? He had a queasy feeling he was yet to discover the true cost.

Later he went back to his office at the old SPB building. He tried to tell himself that life had to go on, but it was hard. He leafed through a bunch of architects' resumes without really seeing them, his thoughts still on Zella. It had seemed to him that she'd turned a corner somehow. Matured, found some measure of peace with herself. She'd thrown herself into life with a new enthusiasm. And now . . .

He looked around and wondered if the Foundation had been worth it. If he'd never come into the Thornhills' lives would things have worked out differently?

His computer cleared its electronic throat. He'd programmed it to do that every time mail came in. Now he turned his attention to the screen and punched up his inbox. The new email read:

**Worry about your own safety.
The dead can take care of themselves.
A Fly on the Wall.**

His temper snapped and he slammed his fist on the desk. Goddammit, who was sending these crank emails?

His phone buzzed. It was Mallory. 'Hello?'

'Jack? Can you get over to my office right now?'

'Sure. Why?'

'Just get here — quickly.'

She ended the call.

He sagged. Now what? He grabbed his jacket, got in the Camaro and drove straight to Graham Towers. When he entered Mallory's office he saw she had visitors — Lieutenant Isaacs and another cop with unruly black hair who introduced himself as Detective Diaz.

Before Jack could say anything, Mallory said: 'Can you believe this shit? I'm actually a suspect in Zella's death!'

'Everyone's a suspect, Mrs. Thornhill,' Lieutenant Isaacs said diplomatically. 'It's just routine.' As if to prove it, he turned to

Jack and said: 'Where were you between seven and ten this morning, Professor?'

Jack frowned. 'Uhm . . . I went for a run, got home, showered, grabbed a coffee at Starbucks on Van Ness, then later, at the Foundation with Mr. and Mrs. Thornhill.'

'I already told them that,' Mallory said. 'I know it was almost ten because my husband had to leave for a meeting. Check with his secretary, she'll verify what I'm saying.'

'I already have, ma'am. It was with his trainer at the stables.' Isaacs looked at Jack. 'One last thing, sir: between Starbucks and meeting Mr. and Mrs. Thornhill at the Foundation — that's probably what, an hour unaccounted for?'

'About that, I guess.'

'Can you tell me what you were doing during that time?'

'I uh . . . called my secretary to make sure none of my appointments had been cancelled . . . Oh, yeah, and I talked to my associate, Jilly Ingram, for a few minutes at the hospital . . . to see how she was doing.'

'Thank you, sir. We'll check on that. Goodbye, Professor. Mrs. Thornhill.'

After they left, Mallory glared sourly at Jack. 'First you suspect me of trying to kill Jilly, now Homicide's accusing me of murdering Zella . . . I feel like some kind of crotch-sniffing serial killer.'

'Calm down. You heard him: It's just routine.'

'Maybe to them, not to me. I'm scared, Jack. What's going on? Is some psycho trying to kill everyone connected to the Foundation? 'Cause if so, one of us — you, me or Brady — is next!'

★　★　★

At the Four Seasons Training Stables, located just off Eastshore Highway, Brady Thornhill, Max Harriwell and Alec Frye stood at the fence and watched a beautiful chestnut colt race around the exercise track. Though Brady wore a black armband in mourning for his dead daughter, he looked anything but unhappy as he clicked his stopwatch and then checked the horse's time.

'Twenty-two and change for a quarter! Still sorry you bought in, Max?'

The fat businessman took the cigar from between his fleshy lips and said: 'Ask me that again after Bay Meadows.'

Frye's cell buzzed. He checked the caller ID, then excused himself and stepped to one side. 'Yeah?'

Mallory said: 'That little package we discussed. Was it delivered?'

'Of course.'

'Then make the call.'

Frye glanced around to make sure he was out of earshot, then said: 'You sure about this?'

'What, now you're my conscience? Just make the fucking call.'

'All r— '

The line went dead.

Frye thought for a moment, then punched in another number.

* * *

It was late afternoon, and Jack was poring over blueprints while the last of the remodeling work went on around him. It had been a long day and he was still thinking about Jilly and Zella when a shadow fell across his plans. Startled, he looked up.

'Wha — oh, it's you.'

Lieutenant Isaacs exchanged a look with his Hispanic partner before saying: 'I wonder if you'd mind letting us look in your car, sir?'

Jack frowned. 'What for?'

'Just routine, Professor. Of course, if you'd like us to get a warrant . . . ?'

'No need for that.'

He led them to the back of the building, where a long row of cars occupied the parking places. Handing his keys to Isaacs, he stood back while they put on latex gloves and then searched through the Camaro. A few moments later Isaacs' partner said: 'Lieutenant . . . '

He held up Zella's thong-panties.

'Where?' asked Isaacs.

'Behind the passenger seat.'

Isaacs said: 'Bag 'em.' Then, to Jack: 'Mind telling me who those belong to?'

Shocked, Jack finally managed to say:

'I'd be happy to, if I knew.'

'Could they be Zella Thornhill's?'

'Not in a million years.'

'Then you and she weren't . . . ?'

'Lovers? No way.'

Detective Diaz held the bag up as if it were a bizarre trophy. 'DNA'll tell us,' he said. 'Looks like this bad boy's got semen all over it.'

Jack felt sick. 'Am I under arrest, Lieutenant?'

'Not yet. But we'll need your DNA.'

'Sure. *After* I talk to my lawyer.'

Isaacs gave him a cool smile. 'You do that, Professor. But once you're through talking, don't make yourself hard to find.'

19

Jack went directly to Thornhill's penthouse office and told him what had happened. Thornhill listened in grim silence and then said: 'I appreciate your telling me this in person, Jack, but you needn't have bothered. I know you and Zella weren't, uh . . . ' He waved one hand in a meaningless gesture, too upset to finish.

'Well, I didn't want you to hear it first from the cops.'

'Then you do think the panties are hers?'

'Gut instinct? Yes.'

'Which means someone planted them.'

'The same 'someone' who rammed her car into the Bay and Jilly into that trench.'

'Why? What's the connection?'

'I don't know. Mallory thinks it's the Foundation, but I don't buy that. But whoever's behind it is trying to frame me for murder.'

'You're gonna need a lawyer,' Thornhill decided. He reached for a pen and scribbled down a number. 'Call Cy Wald. He's an arrogant prick, but if I was jammed up for a murder, I'd want him representing me.'

'Thanks.'

* * *

When Cy Wald arrived at the SPB building that evening, Jack went through everything again. At the end of it Wald broke his long silence. 'You did the right thing, Professor. Never give the cops anything without a court order.'

That was scant comfort. 'If it turns out they're Zella's panties,' he asked, 'can they arrest me?'

'You let me worry about that. From now on I do all your thinking and all your talking. You don't take a piss without asking me first if it's okay. Clear?'

'As glass.'

No sooner had the attorney left than Alec Frye called. 'We need to talk,' he told Jack. 'Meet me at the *End Zone*.'

Remembering what the lawyer had just told him, Jack hesitated. Then he thought about Jilly, and Zella, and deciding he'd been passive too long, said: 'I'm on my way.'

When he arrived at the *End Zone* he found Frye waiting for him in a corner booth and joined him, Coors Lite in hand.

'I checked with a buddy of mine on the force,' said Frye. 'Word is, Lieutenant Isaacs got an anonymous tip about the panties being in your car.'

'No surprises there, then.'

'You think it's her, don't you? Mallory.'

Jack shrugged and took a long swig of cold beer. 'Do the math. It's not you or Jilly, and my gut says it isn't Brady. That only leaves Mallory.'

'But what's her motive? I thought you said she was using the Foundation as a springboard into the governor's mansion?'

'Yeah, but the Foundation's a lock now. We've finished interviewing candidates for the grants. All that's left is to make our final selection. Once that's done,

Mallory's home free.' He paused as a thought hit him, then added: 'Come to think of it, she'd get more notoriety if I was out of the way . . . Man, talk about being sucked in.'

Frye seemed to share his unease, but then he was a very good actor. 'You're kiddin' me, right?' he said. 'You didn't really buy into that connivin' nympho's sweet talk?' Jack's guilty look said it all. 'Oh man-n-n . . . Not you! You're a fuckin' professor. Brains up the gazoo. You couldn't be that fuckin' stupid . . . '

'My Ph.D. didn't come from between my legs.'

'No, but if Brady ever finds out about you'n her, he'll sure as hell cut off what's hanging there.'

Jack drained his glass. 'Thanks, Al. You've been a real comfort.'

★   ★   ★

Mallory was waiting for him when he got back to his office in the SPB building. The moment he came through the door she smiled her killer smile and said:

217

'Brady just called from the funeral home. He wants you to join us for dinner tonight.'

'Thanks, but I'm really not up for it.'

'You have to be. He wants to go over the plans for the Grand Opening ceremony next Saturday at the Fairmont.'

'Business as usual, huh?'

She shrugged, immune to his sarcasm. 'Life goes on, Jack.'

'So they say. But I know how much he loved Zella. I thought her death would be the only thing on his mind right now.'

'You don't know Brady. He gets through tough times by burying himself in his work or his hobbies.' She was silent briefly, then said: 'Please say yes. He's your friend, Jack, and right now he needs you.' She moved closer, wrapped her arms around his neck and kissed him. '*I* need you, too.'

She reached for his belt but he pushed her hands away.

'What, you don't want me anymore?'

She kissed him again. His resistance weakened. Then her cell buzzed and they broke apart, she reluctantly, he with relief.

She checked the caller ID and angrily took the call. 'What is it?'

Alec Frye said: 'If you want to kill him, it's gotta be tonight.'

'Why?'

'I was at the stables. I heard Brady telling the trainer that right after the funeral he's flying to London.'

She moved away from Jack before continuing. 'London?' she said quietly. 'No way. He would've told me. He knows I need time to pack.'

'Who says you're goin' along for the ride?'

She frowned. 'He's not taking me?'

'Not unless you want to share him with Alice.'

Mallory bristled. 'That dumb bitch isn't even bright enough to be a model.'

'Bright enough to be banging your old man right under your fuckin' nose, though,' said Frye, and the way he said it showed just how much fun payback could be.

'All right,' she said through gritted teeth. 'Tonight it is. Tonight he dies.'

Jack arrived at the manse in Pacific Heights at the appointed time, and was ushered into the library. Brady greeted him with his usual gusto, further puzzling Jack with his lack of grief, while Mallory was merely pleasantly polite. The three of them enjoyed a pre-dinner drink before the large Jacobean fireplace before leaving for the restaurant.

By any stretch, the mansion was magnificent. 'I didn't know it at the time,' said Mallory, 'but Brady'd had his eye on this house even before we were married. It wasn't for sale then, but my husband has enough bulldog in him not to let go once he grabs hold of something. And later, when we were on our honeymoon, the realtor called and said the property was back on the market. Brady said buy it, and when I asked him what he'd just bought he said — '

' — I said: 'What *we've* just bought,'' said Brady. 'She said: 'Okay, what did *we* just buy?' and I put my arms around her and said: 'Our own private acre of paradise.''

Wishing he were anywhere else than here, Jack said politely: 'Well, you sure got *that* right.'

At last they left the house, climbed into the awaiting limousine and drove to the restaurant Brady had chosen. He was trying to be a good host, but Jack could tell his heart wasn't really in it and decided that maybe Mallory had been right after all: that this was just his way of getting through it, of trying to keep things ticking over as if nothing had happened.

As the mansion fell behind them Brady hit a button on his console and told the chauffeur on the other side of the black glass screen to swing by the stables first.

'This won't take long,' he told Jack. 'A horse Max Harriwell and I own might have a viral infection. He's running at Bay Meadows day after tomorrow and I want to check on him.'

Forty minutes later they took a left just past Eastshore State Park. Brady explained that a number of stables were located along this curve in the bay between Richmond Inner Harbor and the Berkeley Yacht Harbor — hardly a surprise when you realized that Golden Gate Fields was almost right next door.

The limo followed an access road between white-painted corral fences until a line of silhouetted box stalls and paddocks came into sight. The chauffeur pulled up before he reached them, and Brady got out, urging Jack and Mallory to do likewise. The night was quiet, cool, clear. Brady led them to the stalls.

Alerted by the sound of Brady's arrival, the horse's trainer, a small man with a once-broken nose, came out of the end stall and greeted him. Brady nodded toward the chestnut inside. 'How's he doing?'

'Better. He's responding well, but it's still too early to say if he can run on Saturday. Vet said it looked encouraging, though.'

'Well, that's something. Thanks for staying on, Jimbo. You can go home now.'

The trainer tipped his hat to Mallory and walked off into the darkness. Watching him go, Thornhill said: 'Guess I overreacted. Sorry I dragged you guys out here.'

'No problem,' Jack said.

As they returned to the car, the driver's door opened and the chauffeur got out. Except that it wasn't the chauffeur. It was Alec Frye . . . and he had a gun in his right fist.

Jack frowned. 'Al! What's going on?'

Frye glanced at Mallory and said: 'Tell them.'

20

She was delighted to. Smiling coolly at Jack she said: 'You and Brady, you got into a jealous fight over me and you ended up shooting him.'

'*What?*'

It was Brady, his voice heavy with disbelief.

'Then you tried to shoot me,' she went on, fixing Jack with a too-bright stare. 'But Alec fired first, killing you.'

Heart hammering, Jack said: 'How convenient. And just before I died, I bet I confessed to killing Zella?'

'That won't fly,' growled Brady. 'Why would Jack kill her? You guys were buddies, not lovers.'

'That's not what the police will think when DNA proves his joy juice is all over her panties,' said Mallory.

'What'd you do,' asked Jack, disgusted. 'Scrape it off the sheets?'

'Something like that.'

'Zella's right,' he said. 'You *are* a piece of work.'

'I warned you not to fuck her,' Brady pointed out.

Jack nodded. 'Yes, you did. And now it looks like I'm gonna pay for it.' He looked at Frye just as Frye looked at Thornhill, and suddenly it all became clear. 'Or *am* I? Sonofabitch! Brady, you're beautiful.'

'What're you talking about?' Mallory demanded.

'The perfect double-cross,' Jack said. 'Man, what a putz I've been. Don't you get it, Mallory? Alec told you I needed financing for my Foundation. You saw me as a great way to get rid of your husband. But who do you think told Alec to hook up with me in the first place?' When she didn't answer, he added: 'If I hadn't been so wrapped up in the Foundation, I would've caught on earlier: a hardcore baseball fan hanging out in a football junkie bar called the *End Zone*. Coincidence? I don't think so.'

'Alec . . . ?' began Mallory.

Frye ignored her and looked at Thornhill for orders.

'C'mon, Brady,' said Jack. 'Don't let him just *hang* there.'

Thornhill said to Frye: 'All right. Go ahead. I've heard enough.'

Relieved, Frye aimed his gun at Jack and Mallory. Mallory said: 'What're you doing?'

'Getting ready to kill us,' Jack said grimly. 'He's Brady's man, Mallory. Always has been.'

Mallory whirled angrily on her husband. 'You devious bastard! You let me hang myself, didn't you?'

'It's the only way I could cut loose from you without being taken to the cleaners,' he replied. Then turning to Jack: 'I'm curious, Prof. What gave me away?'

'When you mentioned Max Harriwell. Even billionaires have to talk about something over their cigars and cognac. My guess is he told you about our meeting and you took it from there.'

'Close. Actually, I heard about you first. When Max said he was meeting with you, I asked him to make his terms unacceptable, so you'd walk away. Then I had Alec here move in on you. The rest, as they say, is history.'

'So now what?'

'You two lovebirds disappear. I leak a rumor that you're living in Rio . . . and act like my heart is broken.'

'Think the cops'll buy that?'

'They will when my lawyers explain how you ran off with the Foundation funds.'

'Funds that will 'magically' end up in your pocket?'

Thornhill shrugged. 'It's called a win-win situation.' Then, all at once, his face got ugly and he snapped to Frye: 'Do it.'

Frye coldly aimed his gun at Jack. 'No hard feelin's, I hope . . . '

Before he could pull the trigger a shot came from the direction of the stables. Frye turned to face this new threat and a second shot blasted the darkness.

'*Drop it!*' a voice ordered.

Recognizing it, Frye did just that.

A moment later Zella came out of the shadows, a .38 in her right hand, smoke trailing from the snub-nosed barrel.

Jack and Mallory stared at her in disbelief.

Thornhill glared at Zella. 'What the hell are you doing?'

'Rewriting the finale,' she said. Glancing at Jack she added: 'When I agreed to play dead so he could nail Mallory, he never said he was going to kill you.'

'I'm glad that made a difference,' he said sourly.

'I wanted to tell you I was alive but Dad said you wouldn't go along with it . . . I knew it was wrong but I couldn't let her go on hurting people . . . ruining their lives.'

Mallory had heard enough. Seizing the moment, she pulled a 9mm automatic from her purse — the same weapon Zella had found in her underwear drawer. She didn't waste time on words — she just aimed the weapon at Brady and went to pull the trigger.

Zella screamed. At the same instant Jack threw himself at Mallory. The gun went off, a white muzzle-flare shooting upward, then she fell backward under his weight.

They grappled on the ground, and though he struggled to get a grip on her she was enraged now and managed to rake his face with her nails. As he tried to grab her wrist, she twisted her gun-hand free of his and once again fired the weapon.

This time she hit her target — and Zella collapsed.

As she fell, the rage that had given Mallory strength now consumed Brady. He leapt to his daughter's side, wrenched the .38 from her lifeless fingers, thrust it toward Mallory and —

Jack's eyes went wide and in the second before Brady fired the first bullet he quickly rolled sideways. The bullet slammed into Mallory, knocking her flat. Though she was already dead, Brady kept firing, pumping round after round into her until he ran out of bullets.

Stunned by the violence, Jack got to his feet and stumbled over to Zella. He knelt beside her, cradling her head. She stirred weakly in his arms. 'Brady!' he yelled. 'Brady! For God's sake, she's still alive!'

His shout penetrated Brady's rage and

he came running over. Kneeling beside Jack he leaned close to Zella and clutching her hand, begged her to, 'Hang on, Princess . . . please, baby . . . hang on . . . ' And then, to Frye: 'Call 9-1-1!'

★ ★ ★

Quicker than Jack thought possible everyone was on the scene: the police, the Alameda County sheriff/coroner, in whose jurisdiction things had come to a head, the paramedics . . . and, because it involved the Thornhills, the media.

Zella received treatment for her shoulder-wound at the scene, and after that she was placed on a gurney, lifted into the attending ambulance and rushed off to the closest ER. Brady insisted on riding with her.

All Mallory got was a body bag and a one-way ride to the Alameda County morgue.

Lieutenant Isaacs showed up along with his partner, Diaz. The big black detective looked from Jack to Frye and said: 'So — which one of you wants to tell me what went down here?'

'We'll be happy to give you a statement — ' began Frye.

' — after we've spoken to our lawyers,' added Jack.

Isaacs again looked at each man in turn. Finally he said: 'I can't wait to get *that* on record.' He and Diaz moved off to their car.

'Look,' Frye said to Jack, 'I'm sorry I couldn't clue you in before, but — '

Jack hit him. Frye went sprawling, mouth bloodied, eyes filled with surprise and anger.

'That's for Jilly,' Jack said softly.

'That was a mistake, for chrissake!' said Frye, struggling to his feet. 'I only intended to scare her, but her fuckin' tire blew and — '

Jack hit him again — and this time, when Frye went down, Jack called: 'Lieutenant Isaacs! I want this bastard arrested for trying to kill my associate.'

★　★　★

Next morning Zella was well enough to receive visitors. She made sure the first two were her father and Jack.

In the privacy of her room, she said: 'Okay, here's the deal: Jack keeps his Foundation; you keep your money; and I stick to my story about how some drunken, demented truck driver accidently rammed my Ferrari into the Bay.'

Brady sucked in a breath. 'But Princess, Jack and Mallory were — '

'Dad, do you really want to play the injured party here? Or do you want to keep getting richer and go on banging those babes you've got stashed in condos all over the city?'

He looked as if he'd been doused in ice-water. 'You know about that . . . ?'

'You'd be surprised how much I know about you, Dad. So would the media. Especially after you shot your wife — '

' — in self-defense.'

'Do you really think the tabloids will care about that? They'll print whatever sells best and worry about lawsuits later.'

He knew that was true, so he said softly: 'Okay . . . you win.'

'Nobody wins, Thornhill,' said Jack,

finally breaking his long silence. 'We just get another chance to play the game, that's all.'

★ ★ ★

The game went on the following Saturday night, when guests from San Francisco's elite attended the grand opening of the Monroe Foundation at the Fairmont Hotel.

Thornhill spared no expense. He chose the swankiest location, hired the finest seven-piece band, the food was excellent and the alcohol flowed freely from bottles that cost eighty dollars a throw.

About an hour into the festivities Thornhill finally took the stage and addressed his guests. 'Let me have your attention, ladies and gentlemen . . . I'm not gonna bore you with a long speech — I'll let Professor Monroe do that.'

He gestured for Jack to join him. Reluctantly Jack did so.

'Folks,' Thornhill continued, 'it's my pleasure and my honor to introduce the man of the hour, the man responsible for reminding me that the future of this great country lies in the hands of dedicated young visionaries who deserve to be nurtured so that their architectural dreams can be fulfilled, for only then will the world benefit from their extraordinary talent. My friends — Professor Jack Monroe!'

Applause erupted from the audience. Thornhill stepped back from the mic and indicated that Jack should say a few words. Jack hesitated, remembering all the anxiety dreams he'd had leading to this moment. All at once he was back there on the stage in his dreams, blinded by spotlights and wondering what in hell he was going to say.

At last he cleared his throat. 'Somebody famous once said that home was where you hang your architect. I guess whoever said it had had a pretty bad experience with one. And let's not kid ourselves, folks. God knows He's a great architect, but all too many architects believe they're even greater than God. What we should remember — indeed, what we should never *forget* — is that architecture is all about function, structure and beauty, and that it should always be created to serve the needs of the people for whom it is intended. These are the basic tenets of architecture, beliefs which sadly and all too often are sacrificed for the ego of those who think they know better. At the Monroe Foundation, however, these are the four goals we will always strive to teach, achieve and above all *respect*.'

There was more applause. When it quieted down, Jack said, simply: 'The Foundation would never have come about but for my father, Jake Monroe. He had exceptional ideas and great imagination. What he didn't have was money and opportunity.

'Well, there's not much we can do about the money, but we can certainly offer the opportunity.' He swallowed, then added: 'This is for you, Dad.'

He left the stage to thunderous applause and hurried through the throng until he reached Zella and Jilly. Although Zella's left arm hung in a sling, it did little to take away just how stunning she looked in her glittery-blue one-shoulder evening dress. But right then he only had eyes for Jilly, who was in a wheelchair at their table.

'Woof!' he said. 'You guys look hot!'

'Well,' said Zella, gesturing to Jilly, 'what're you waiting for? Ask the lady to dance.'

'What about you?'

'I'll be a 'fly on the wall',' she replied.

For a moment Jack didn't catch on. Then, as it hit him: 'Those emails? They came from you? Jesus! Why didn't you just tell me?'

'I tried to ... that day in your apartment when I told you not to take Dad's money.'

'Couldn't you have been more obvious?'

'Not without implicating Dad and maybe letting Mallory off the hook,' she said grimly. 'It's not easy being stuck in the middle, you know.'

He smiled and reached over to give her a careful hug. Then he turned to Jilly and to her alarm, scooped her up out of her chair.

'J-Jack, no . . . no, don't . . . '

He silenced her with a kiss, to which she immediately responded. It was the kind of kiss that can knock a man's socks off — and that was just how Jack felt as he carried her out onto the dance floor.

Zella watched the other dancers clear a space for them and her face sobered briefly with envy. Then a voice behind her said: 'Thirsty, love?'

As she turned around, Rosy sat down beside her with two flutes of champagne. Zella took one and smiled. 'Thanks. Enjoying yourself?'

Rosy shrugged. 'All I need is a little encouragement.'

They locked gazes, and to her surprise Zella felt a connection she'd never felt before. 'I've just bought a new Ferrari that would love to stretch its legs,' she said cautiously.

Rosy grinned. 'Drink up, then . . . and after that you can show me exactly what she can do.'

On the dance floor, Jack saw them leave together. Then a new thought occurred to him. 'Whatever happened to your boy-friend?' he asked Jilly.

'He's finally beginning to notice me,' she said, straight-faced.

Jack shook his head. Do me a favor? Tell him he's an idiot for taking so long.'

'You're an idiot,' she said.

Grinning, he swirled her around again.

THE END

We do hope that you have enjoyed reading this large print book.

Did you know that all of our titles are available for purchase?

We publish a wide range of high quality large print books including:

Romances, Mysteries, Classics
General Fiction
Non Fiction and Westerns

Special interest titles available in large print are:

The Little Oxford Dictionary
Music Book, Song Book
Hymn Book, Service Book

Also available from us courtesy of Oxford University Press:

Young Readers' Dictionary
(large print edition)
Young Readers' Thesaurus
(large print edition)

For further information or a free brochure, please contact us at:
Ulverscroft Large Print Books Ltd.,
The Green, Bradgate Road, Anstey,
Leicester, LE7 7FU, England.
Tel: (00 44) **0116 236 4325**
Fax: (00 44) **0116 234 0205**

THE HEEL OF ACHILLES

Gerald Verner

'I'm done for . . . find X.1 . . . Dene . . . You must . . .Tooth-paste . . . ' England is at war with Germany and Dene of the Secret Service tries to decipher his fatally wounded colleague's garbled message — potentially vital information for England's survival. Who is X.1? What does the word *Tooth-paste* signify? Dene must find out and stop X.1, or the Third Reich will strike a crippling blow to England and change the course of the war. And he has just eight days in which to do it . . .

DEAD SECRET

Gerald Verner

Criminologist Felix Heron and his wife, Thelma, investigate Sir Percival Trench's death on the hunting field. The inquest's verdict is that it was an accident, but his fiancée thinks otherwise. The case becomes increasingly complex, not least when it appears that Sir Percival's fortune of two hundred and twenty thousand pounds has vanished. Then, when the dead body of a 'grass' is found hanging on a tree — Heron has plenty to work on before finding an unexpected solution.